*Totally Bound Publishing books by Aurora Russell*

**Single Books**
The Au Pair and the Beast

**Anywhere and Always**
Falling for the Tycoon
Snowbound with the Billionaire
Guarded by a Hero

**Minne-sorta Falling in Love**
Semper Fitz

Anywhere and Always

# GUARDED BY A HERO

## AURORA RUSSELL

Guarded by a Hero
ISBN # 978-1-80250-969-4
©Copyright Aurora Russell 2022
Cover Art by Erin Dameron-Hill ©Copyright August 2022
Interior text design by Claire Siemaszkiewicz
Totally Bound Publishing

Published in 2022 by Totally Bound Publishing, United Kingdom.

# GUARDED BY
# A HERO

# Dedication

First and always, to my own grumpy hero and our two little gremlins…er, I mean sons.
You guys bring me joy, every single day.
To my dad and stepmom. Your unwavering support and love have always lifted me up, making me a better person and writer.
To my brother and sister-in-law and their two munchkins.
No amount of distance can ever truly separate us.
To my unbelievable friends. I know I have the best friends in the world when I laugh so hard my cheeks and stomach hurt after every visit.
To my amazing in-laws. You show us every day how much you care for and support us.
Last — but most certainly not least — this book is for my fans. Each kind word, comment, review and recommendation is profoundly appreciated.

# Chapter One

*Nine months earlier*

The fête was truly lovely, a great mix of elegance and charm, and Clothilde might have been enjoying herself if her hip, leg and back hadn't ached so damn much. She knew she shouldn't have stayed so long — and she particularly should have found a way to avoid dancing — but she'd wanted to ensure that Rémy's friend, Annelise, had a good time. She used the term 'friend' liberally, since her brother's relationship with the young American event planner was obviously much more romantic and complex than mere friendship. To help Rémy, she'd needed to draw Charles Pinkston, Annelise's boss, away.

Without conceit, she knew that she was a woman who men considered to be very beautiful, and it seemed that even the pain she'd suffered since the accident hadn't lessened her appeal too much. And so, to give Rémy and Annelise more time together without the older man's kindly interference, she had danced with Charles twice, as well as completing several circuits of the ballroom with him. Later, she'd made an additional full tour of the party with Annelise alone, introducing the American to some of Montreal's young elite. Luckily, a number of her close friends had been in attendance, including Pauline Cartouchel and Élodie Carillon. Both women would be excellent for Annelise to claim as acquaintances in Montreal society.

Now Clothilde's feet weren't thanking her but were aching in their stylish, strappy heels, shoes which she would have worn without a second thought only a year ago. Worse, though, putting her body under the strain of wearing heels and staying active for so long had made her newly healed muscles and bones positively throb with pain, like a hot flame was crawling up from the balls of her feet into her left leg, hip and now along her spine.

She tried to hide a grimace under a flirtatious smile, and she must have succeeded, because Charles Pinkston finally, blessedly, said a charming good evening to her, kissing her hand. He was such a sweet man, who obviously missed his late wife terribly. She held herself still for a moment as she watched him walk toward the door before allowing her shoulders to droop just a little bit to ease some of the stiffness that she knew she was going to pay hell for over the next several days. She froze as she swore she could almost feel the heat of disapproval from behind her. *Marc Constantin.*

She felt his approach more than heard him, like a big predator, stalking on silent feet.

"You'd better sit down before you fall down, Duchess." His tone was hard and angry, but there was an underlying tenderness. *Or maybe I just wish there was* — which she knew was ridiculous, since as her bodyguard, it was his job to watch out for her. Literally, taking care of her physical well-being was in the job description. Yet she felt goosebumps rise on the wealth of bare skin on her chest, arms and back, exposed by the daring cut of the dress. When she turned her head to look at him, his dark blue eyes blazed with some strong emotion.

"I'm fine," she answered, her tone clipped.

He raised one pale eyebrow, his skepticism obvious.

"Right. Is that why, when you think no one's watching, you look like one strong puff of air would make you topple over?"

She turned fully toward him, drawing her annoyance around her like a cape.

"I'm having a *wonderful* time," she insisted, even as her joints burned with protest. "Didn't anyone tell you? I'm a total social butterfly, the darling of Montreal society. That's what all the gossip sites say." She didn't know what about Marc Constantin made her so desperate to goad him, but she couldn't help herself. Regardless of her bright tone, though, her left leg and hip, the side that had taken the brunt of her car accident six months earlier, began to tremble, in spite of her best efforts. She hoped that the tremors were so subtle that Marc wouldn't notice, but she should have known better.

"Screw this. I'm calling for the car and we're sitting down *now*," he pronounced and took her elbow with a growl, leading her toward one of the quiet alcoves in the tastefully decorated hallway just outside the ballroom. Anyone looking at them would have seen a well-dressed security guard very properly escorting a beautiful young woman in an evening gown, albeit perhaps a little closely. But while Marc's grip wasn't painful, it was firm and unrelenting, with no give at all.

*Much like the man himself,* she mused. She was too damn tired to fight his hold, anyway, considering she'd been dreaming of sitting down on one of the cushioned benches herself for at least the past hour.

The relief from the pressure on her joints was instant and profound as he settled her on the thickly padded bench, and she had to stifle a groan of pleasure. Surprising her, he slid in next to her, so close she could feel the heat that he continually seemed to give off. Surreptitiously, she inhaled his rich, fresh masculine scent. He always smelled like he had just come in from outdoors, even when she knew he'd been inside for hours. He turned the focus of his angry gaze on her again.

"Why do you let them tell you how to act?" he asked, but it sounded more like a demand.

Clothilde narrowed her eyes.

"That question is totally inappropriate," she huffed.

He looked unrepentant. "I notice you didn't deny it."

She stared straight ahead, unwilling to acknowledge his comment. She was done answering to anyone, especially any man not related to her. Since her relationship had ended with her childhood sweetheart and ex-fiancé, Claude—Claude, who had wanted to tell her what to wear, who to meet, how to act—she had vowed never to diminish herself for another man again.

His posture relaxed infinitesimally, and some of the anger on his face seemed to fade, replaced by resignation.

"Keep your secrets, then. But answer this… Do your brothers even understand what it costs you to pretend to be normal so they don't feel so bad?"

Clothilde couldn't help turning to look at him in surprise at his softly spoken question and the understanding behind it. Normally, she would continue to refuse to answer or tell him he was way off base. This time, something in his eyes, so warm and understanding, was too compelling to ignore.

"I don't want them to know," she admitted. "It was so hard for them when I was miserable, then when I almost died, it was breaking their hearts. I want them to think that I'm normal. They *deserve* a normal, happy sister." It felt good to say the words out loud — and even better to say them to Marc.

He was silent for a long moment, then laid one large, scarred hand on top of her pale, smooth one where it lay on the table. "You don't have to keep up the act with me, Duchess."

It was funny, but the sarcastic nickname he'd given her the first day they'd met sounded more and more like an endearment now.

"I…ah…I speak from experience when I say that if you keep playin' a role for everyone, you're gonna to lose something you might not be able to get back."

A dull flush rose in Marc's tan cheeks, and he looked uncomfortable, as if he regretted saying so much. The urge to ask him to tell her more about himself practically tugged at her lips, but she tried to fight it. Up until that moment, she'd gotten the sense that asking Marc anything at all about himself was completely off-limits. From the background check her family had run before hiring him, she knew he was American and ex-military. He'd recently left the service with high honors, and he'd been married and divorced years earlier. Even without the background check, she would have recognized he was from Boston, from the accent that was usually faint but which became stronger when he was angry. But he'd never volunteered anything else.

"Is that what happened to you?" she asked, almost in spite of herself.

He rubbed the back of his neck uncomfortably, and his jaw hardened. "Shouldn't have said anything. Forget it. Go ahead and push yourself until you drop." As he spoke, his tone became terser until he was almost spitting the words. He hadn't removed his other hand from hers, and his grip grew harsh.

He started to get up, and she knew she should let him, but she just couldn't allow him to walk away with that cold, angry expression on his face. After months of watching each other, and exchanging pointed remarks, she didn't want him to leave their first real conversation like this.

"Fine...forget I asked. It's none of my business. Just don't go away angry," she said softly, and he halted his movements. "*Please*," she added, when he still seemed frozen in indecision.

He sat back down heavily, and deep satisfaction flared in her chest. No, it was more than that. She felt the warmth of a tentative truce, and maybe something more...like the beginnings of friendship.

"I know you don't like me, Marc—"

His harsh laugh interrupted her.

"Don't *like* you?" His smile was humorless, but no less devastating. "Is *that* what you think?"

Confusion rose inside her, and she didn't even try to hide it.

"Of course. It's obvious. I mean, I know you're committed to your job, but everything you say... I can tell that I irritate you." She paused, thinking back over all the pointed barbs over the past few months, the way his eyes followed her, stormy blue-gray and angry. "The way you talk, the way you look at me, as if you loathe me sometimes—"

He was shaking his head, and there was something else in his expression that she'd never seen before. "No, sweetheart."

She was as shocked by his gentle tone as by his calling her 'sweetheart', which sounded more like *sweet-haht* with his accent.

"I should let you keep thinking that, but...I want you to know the truth. Well, some of the truth anyway." His laugh was dry. When he looked at her again, his eyes glowed in the dim light. "I don't loathe you. I look at you because you're so fuckin' beautiful, like a goddamn star from the sky."

Her mind reeled, unable to process what he was saying. "But you hate touching me... You pull your hand away," she whispered.

He leaned closer and trailed one hand, work-roughened and scratchy, down her bare shoulder. She shivered.

"I pull back because I like touching you too damn much." His voice was a low growl now, and she should have been wary, but instead she felt comforted — warm and safe in a way she hadn't felt in a long time. He was a large man, tall and broad, with blunt features that individually might have been too harsh, but which combined were undeniably compelling. He had a magnetism, at least for her, so that she couldn't turn away from his rough, masculine beauty.

She was so close to him that she could feel the vibrations of his phone in his pocket as it went off. He coughed uncomfortably as he took it out, breaking the spell.

"Car's out of the side door," he said. He was so ridiculously careful of her, doing things like arranging for the car to come to an unexpected door instead of the front. She'd always thought he was just thorough at his job — and he certainly was that — but now she wondered if there was more to it.

She gave a curt nod and wiggled her way out of the alcove, feeling a flare of heat at the slight pressure of his hand on her bare arm. He must have signaled the attendant to bring their coats, and he slid hers on with aching tenderness that made her heartbeat speed. Walking again, after too short a break, made her body scream, her nerve endings sizzling with pain. She took carefully measured steps, one after another, breathing through the worst of it, but Marc must have sensed it anyway as he held her arm more firmly, lending her some of his strength. She shot him a grateful smile, but his face was like a thundercloud as they stepped outside into the icy night air. The side alley was relatively quiet, but someone in a dark overcoat, so bundled up that she couldn't tell if it was a man or a woman, hurried by just as the driver was opening the door of the sleek black sedan, jostling her into it.

At the contact of her bad side with the hard metal, she felt a jolt of pain so intense that it stole her breath so she could only make a muffled whimper of sound, and her eyes filled with tears.

"Goddamn it," Marc growled, his tone one of icy fury, but the harshness of his voice was offset by the tenderness of his movements as he lifted her to settle her into the car. He crouched down, looking torn between going after the stranger who had carelessly pushed her and staying by her side.

"Shit, sweetheart, that looked like it hurt. Are you okay?"

The genuine concern in his voice was her undoing. She tried to nod, to reassure him, but suddenly, all of it was too much. As the pain swept through her, turning her cold then prickly with heat, it overwhelmed all the careful defenses she'd so painstakingly erected during her long recovery. She felt something hot on her face, and reached up to touch the tears in surprise.

"I don't know why I'm crying," she murmured, honestly confused. "I never cry anymore, at least not where anyone can see me. It just seems to make everyone feel worse."

"Aw, sweetheart, you're killing me." He got into the car, shifting her over with one smooth movement, even as he closed the door and pulled her coat off, and he dragged her to him so that she was sheltered under one massive shoulder, her side pressed all along the warmth of his body. He turned his face into her hair, inhaling deeply. When he spoke again, his voice was low, hoarse with conviction. "You cry as much as you want to."

The rough velvet of his voice, the faint smell of leather from his coat, his warmth and his complete solidity — as if he were an immovable megalith — all blended together to shatter her usual resolve completely. She only had an instant to wonder at the suddenness of the feelings — almost like a drug — before sadness engulfed her entirely. She pressed her face into his chest and sobbed for the pain of her body, which no longer cooperated with her wishes, but also for the dreams she'd lost and the fear she lived with, for the terror that still haunted her every night, every time she got into a car or went next to the river in Montreal that she'd once loved so much. Instead of holding himself stiff, or pulling away, Marc stroked her hair and murmured soothing sounds, his breath warm on her temple.

A mild jolt told her the car had started moving, and she heard Marc raise the partition, saying something about her being hurt at the party. Their driver, Serge,

Aurora Russell

who had known her since she was a little girl, would be worried, but she couldn't seem to stop herself.

She should have felt mortified—she knew she would feel awful about this soon—but instead, a strange calm stole over her, followed by a surprising warmth, centered between her legs.

"Better, sweetheart?" Marc's voice was rough but tender, close to her ear.

"Much," she murmured. "Feels good."

Marc tightened his arms around her. "I shouldn't be holding you like this."

Clothilde pressed closer, nearly climbing onto his lap. Something—maybe his closeness—was intoxicating, and the warm arousal was morphing into something hotter. She pressed her thighs together uncomfortably.

"What about kissing me? Should you do that?" She didn't know where the throaty temptress's voice came from. Sure, she'd indulged in a few secret fantasies about Marc, but she hadn't intended to act on them this way. Now that she'd said it, she couldn't be sorry, though.

"No." Marc's tone was clipped on the one word, and his body tensed.

She stretched so that she could whisper into his ear. "What if I *need* you to?"

The lines of his body were so taut that she could almost feel him fighting against himself.

"Want you, need you, *so badly*..." She nearly whimpered as she rubbed herself against him, suddenly desperate to feel his mouth on hers, his hands all over her. She only had a millisecond to wonder at the sudden urgency before an inferno of need swept through her body.

"Never thought our first kiss would be like this, sweetheart, but God, I've dreamed of it for so long," he ground out. His words seemed to break through the wall of reserve that he always kept up, and he pulled her to him until her softness was crushed to his hardness, surrounded by the strength of his arms, before he slanted his mouth over hers in a kiss that devoured her…claimed her. The kiss was bold and sure but simultaneously protective and caring, just like Marc. His flavor was sweet, with a touch of cinnamon, like the apple-spiced cake he'd eaten earlier. His lips were firm but tender as he sucked and teased, before stroking into her mouth with his tongue on her gasp of pleasure.

Her core had gone molten at the first touch of his mouth, and as he continued, she began to buck her hips against him, craving more contact. A little voice in the back of her mind whispered that she'd never felt like this before—had never been *anything* like this at all, and she was acting utterly out-of-character—but she ignored it, too consumed by how amazing Marc felt.

Her nipples hardened under the thin fabric of her dress, and she pushed them toward him as she twined her arms around his neck, pulling herself so she sat partially on his lap, and he lifted her the rest of the way with one muscular arm. Oddly, her arms felt a bit heavy, so that the movement wasn't as easy as it should have been, but she didn't really care as long as she could get closer. The change in position put her directly on top of the proof of Marc's desire, hard and thick below her, and the feel of him rubbing against her core ratcheted up her arousal to new heights. She couldn't help but give a little shiver against him, making him break off their kiss with a groan.

"Damn, that feels amazing." His voice was strangled, and his eyes were dark with passion as she looked down at his face, before he lowered his head to kiss her neck. It set off a riot of sensation, and she threw her head back, thrusting her breasts toward him in a blatant invitation. They had always been such a challenge—sensitive and so full for her slender frame, her nipples prone to tightening—so that some designers hadn't liked to work with her during her modeling days because of her bosom. Marc's expression as he stared at their bounty, however, was almost feral.

Still, he seemed to rein himself in. "Are you sure you want me to touch you that way, baby?" His words were more of a growl than actual language, and it sent a quiver of need throughout her body.

She didn't have to think. She was starved for his touch, everywhere, and so empty that she was aching. "Need your mouth and hands everywhere," she breathed, nearly whimpering with lust.

"Your wish is my command, Duchess," he answered, his voice harsh with desire, and pulled down the top of her dress, along with the cups of the silky strapless bra she wore, releasing her soft mounds.

"God, been dreamin' of doin' that all night…every fucking night," he confessed, his voice so low that she wasn't sure she was meant to hear it. He dipped his head to lave one nipple and her back bowed as she gave a cry of need.

"Sensitive, hm-m?" he asked.

She nodded shakily in reply. "*Oui*," she whispered.

"Let me try something a little different, then." His voice was gravelly, so sexy that the vibrations alone were giving her goosebumps, but then he gently sucked one nipple into the warm haven of his mouth, and she lost all power of thought. Dimly, she felt him ruck up her long skirt so he could work one large hand to where she needed it the most as she rocked against him, breathless and giving little huffs of air on strangled moans.

"God...you're so wet, you're dripping." Marc's voice was wondering, reverent. She knew that she would have normally been embarrassed by the extent of her blatant lust, but she was beyond the point of caring as Marc circled her bud with exquisite gentleness. Even as light as his touch was, his fingers felt white-hot and set off a wave of sensation so overwhelming that she soared headlong past the point of ecstasy into sheer, mindless bliss, clutching at him helplessly as she exploded, then went nearly limp in the aftermath, her vision seeming to tunnel before it righted itself.

"You're glorious, sweetheart....my God, even if I shouldn't have done that." Marc didn't sound very repentant, and his small smile was self-satisfied.

Clothilde felt amazing, but her mind was starting to feel a little sluggish...confused. "Why not? Did I have too much champagne? Have..." Now it was harder to get the words out. She really must have had too many glasses. Had she? "Have to be...careful," she finished, but she slurred.

Marc's body went rigid underneath hers, but with tension rather than desire. "You only had one glass."

Somewhere, dimly, part of her mind was screaming at her to recognize something, but everything felt fuzzy. "Marc?" she managed, or a word that sounded sort of like his name.

"What is it? What's wrong, Clo?" She couldn't even be happy that he'd finally called her by her nickname since he also sounded distinctly alarmed.

"'s ih bad...'f I can't feel m'legs?"

"Shit...shit, shit, shit!" Marc lifted her off him and ran his hands up and down her sides and along her stomach. "He didn't run into you… He *attacked* you, and I was too much of a motherfucking horny asshole to recognize the signs! Does anything hurt?"

He knocked on the divider and barked at the driver what sounded like an order to take her to the nearest hospital, and the car lurched forward. As he grabbed her to keep her heavy body—why couldn't she lift her limbs?—one of his hands connected with her side and made her whimper.

"Hurts," she moaned. "Don' tell my brothers… 'm'hurt…again."

In the flickering of one of the streetlamps that now seemed to be flying by, she saw an agonized expression on his face that would have made her gasp if she could have gotten enough air.

He pulled the fabric of her dress aside, and his expression hardened. In that instant, he looked every inch a warrior, the hero who had gone into battle countless times and kept going back until the job was done.

"He jabbed you with something, but we'll figure it out." He shook his head. "I'm so sorry, sweetheart. So fucking sorry I touched you and didn't realize…"

She should have been afraid, but the fuzziness was turning into full-on lamb's wool, filling her brain with silence. "S'okay," she slurred, trying to reassure him. It seemed really important, so she forced her lips to form the words. "Forgive you."

His eyes were shiny and anguished in the low light as her vision faded.

# Chapter Two

The only thing worse than the smell of a hospital, Marc thought, was the shitty-ass toilet-water they tried to pass off as coffee. He'd still forced down at least three cups in as many hours in order to stay awake, but that didn't mean he'd liked it. *You'd think a military hospital would do better*, he thought, then mentally corrected himself. No, of course not... Utility was the name of the game, not comfort. Was it warm and caffeinated? Then it was good enough.

*Ah, shit, I'm back in a military hospital...* He shifted uncomfortably in the molded plastic seat that was a truly indescribable shade somewhere between beige and puce. He didn't even want to think about how many regulations he'd violated bringing her to a secret joint Canadian-US military hospital that he wasn't supposed to still have the clearance to know about. But damn it... Although he had been slow on the uptake, once he'd realized she'd been injected, he'd recognized that the symptoms Clothilde had experienced were exactly the same as those sometimes induced by the experimental drug that had just had a shipment stolen. *RK781*. It had been engineered as a possible battlefield sedative, but tests were still ongoing because of both the extreme removal of inhibitions and desire that it caused initially—even though only in a certain percentage of trial participants—and the potential of that side effect being used against the field medics. Now, having seen it in action on Clothilde, he could attest to how powerful and rapid-action it was.

Unfortunately, if a dose was too high, there were very few things that could counteract it. He'd known he stood little chance of convincing a *Montrealais* ER doc to give Clothilde a high-dose of a concoction of strong chemicals based only on his military ID and piss-poor French accent, so he'd had Serge, the Gaspard family driver who'd been assigned to them that night, drop him off in front of the gray, 1960s-era building with a faded sign proclaiming it as *Laboratoires Calvert*. If Serge had thought it was strange to be dropping Marc and the young lady of the Gaspard family off at a nondescript lab at nearly midnight, he was too well-trained to bat an eyelash. Marc groaned as he realized that Serge was a loose end he'd have to tell his boss about. Shit, Menzies was going to be pissed as fuck, but Marc couldn't muster even a glimmer of regret.

The harried-looking female doctor had come out a little while earlier to assure him that, while Clothilde was still under from the powerful drugs in her system, the information he'd provided about the chemical makeup of *RK781* had been invaluable and she was improving rapidly. He'd been so relieved that he'd thought he might actually faint. He, Marc Constantin, the tough kid from Roxbury who'd been nicknamed 'Ironsides' by his team for his steely nerves in every situation, had had to plunk his ass down on a hard row chair to keep from falling over with relief.

Now that he was less worried about Clothilde's physical safety, though, he was guilty as hell... ashamed of himself in a way that he'd never been before. Clothilde, the woman he'd been fighting his wildly inappropriate attraction to from the moment he'd seen her, heard her sassy little side comments, smelled her incomparable scent, had begged him to kiss and touch her, and he'd lost his mind and fallen like a ton of bricks. He'd been watching her every move for the past six months—much more closely than he needed to, probably more than was even within the realm of appropriate—so he should have known that she was acting oddly. It was out-of-character enough for her to have let her guard down to cry, but then to have her practically throw herself at him? *God, I'm the asshole who could have ruled the asshats of Dicktopolis.*

Worse, though...he could still feel the outline of her soft curves against him, her hot core pressed to his lap. He could still taste her lush lips, and he imagined he could even smell her feminine musk on his fingers in spite of multiple hand-washings and the over-whelming antiseptic smell around him. His cock, which had been hard since the first second he'd seen her that night, still ached to finish what they'd started. Moreover, he longed to hold her again—to be in that hospital room with her, holding her hand, brushing her silky hair away from her forehead, calling the goddamn nurse to bring water when her eyelashes fluttered open. He couldn't have that—*ever*. Even if Clothilde thought that was what she wanted—and that was a huge *if*— once she found out the truth about him, she'd fucking hate his guts, almost as much as he might be starting to hate himself for what he was doing...what he had to keep doing.

The appearance of an earnest young man in an Army uniform interrupted his maudlin thoughts. *Just in fucking time. One more minute and I would have moved on to blaming myself for accidentally leaving the door open when I was four and letting my childhood cat, Wiley Whiskers, run outside into traffic.*

"Sir?" The young man's voice was tentative. "You're, uh—"

"You can call me Mr. Constantin," Marc cut him off. "What is it?"

The respect and admiration written plainly on the young man's face was uncomfortable, particularly at the moment.

"There's a secure call for you in Room 27B. This way." The younger soldier was efficient, leading Marc past the nurse's station and down several winding hallways.

The room was nondescript, and Marc took a deep breath before he entered, steeling himself for what was sure to be an uncomfortable conversation with the head of his current program. He couldn't bring himself to think of Menzies as a commanding officer—more of a supervisor with a hell of a lot of clout and clearance. Still, he respected the hell out of Menzies, even while he didn't often like him.

Marc thought the younger soldier would leave immediately, but he was surprised to see the junior officer still standing there as Marc turned to pull the door closed.

"I, uh, just wanted to, uh, say that it's a real honor to meet you, sir...um, Mr. Constantin." The kid's cheeks flushed at his error.

*Christ, was I ever that young?* Marc thought, then reined in the cynicism. Sort of.

"Thanks, Koepke," he answered, reading the man's name off his uniform. "Appreciate your help...and discretion."

The young soldier practically clicked his heels together. "Of course, sir."

When he was gone and the door locked behind him, Marc picked up the phone, pressing on the blinking light of a waiting line.

"What the ever-loving-fuck, Constantin?"

Marc could hear Hamish Menzies's customary bellow before he even got the receiver up to his ear. He didn't pretend to misunderstand.

"I fully acknowledge that it's regrettable, but I had to bring Clothilde Gaspard here, sir. She would have died without swift and customized intervention." Marc tried to imbue his voice with respect and to keep his recitation businesslike, emotionless.

"What the hell kind of shit could a society princess get into that would warrant that kind of intervention?" Marc appreciated that Menzies was at least giving him the chance to explain and hadn't corrected him on forgetting to refer to Clothilde as Target Alpha.

"She was dosed with *RK781*," he said quietly.

The silence on the other end of the line was deafening. "Well, shit on a shingle. This changes the whole operation." Menzies' sigh was heavy, but his tone, when he spoke again, was brisk. "How was it administered? And how did you recognize it?"

"Someone tagged Target Alpha as we exited to the vehicle...injected her side by pushing past her." Marc remembered the dark figure in a trench coat. How the hell had the poisoner known he would use the side door? There had only been about thirty seconds where

Clothilde had been somewhat exposed outside. "I recognized it was *RK781* because the target started displaying some of the, uh, reportable behavioral side effects. I was almost too slow, though. She lost consciousness on our way to this hospital."

The other end of the line was so quiet that Marc feared he'd lost the secure connection, which would suck because he really didn't want to repeat himself. Then Menzies cleared his throat and Marc braced himself for the verbal ass-whooping that he deserved. His boss surprised him, though.

"I'm not going to lie and say that this isn't a shitty development, but I am glad that you recognized the signs at all. I've read the reports. We had some trial losses before the potential side effects became apparent." Menzies sounded almost...sympathetic? Was that even possible?

"I'm going to tell you something else, now, too, Constantin. Secret squirrel."

Marc tensed at the reference to top-secret info.

"The study reports also showed that the subjects — the ones who had intervention in time and survived — generally couldn't remember anything after they started slurring their words. They reported that actions they took before that point were, while a bit out character, entirely of their own choosing. So I'm gonna ask you only once — Are we compromised with Target Alpha?"

It made his gut twist, but Marc mentally replayed the moments they'd spent in the car. The way he'd comforted Clothilde, then it had turned into something so much hotter, wilder. She'd seemed out-of-control, so needy — and goddamn him again for being too bowled over and grateful to question her sudden gift — then she'd gone off like a rocket when he'd touched her.

She'd only started slurring her words afterward, before he'd mentioned the drug.

"Negative," he confirmed. "She'll remember some...atypical behavior, on both our parts, but if the intel is correct, she wouldn't remember that she was given a drug."

"That's something, then." Menzies sounded both thoughtful and regretful. "I understand your feelings on this."

Marc doubted that, but he waited for the man to continue.

"But I know that you also understand how important it is that you remain undercover in your current position with the Gaspard family."

Marc bristled at the implication. "I'm capable of maintaining decorum, and Clothilde would never betray a secret."

"Clothilde, hmm-m?"

Marc remained rigid, knowing he'd already pushed the limit enough by questioning his superior.

"Fine, you know her. Maybe she wouldn't do it...*deliberately*, but that's not a chance we can take. We've put years into this operation — with the backing and frankly, *intense* interest of upper brass — and we have to continue to play the long game to get the Chimère. He or she is too smart, too well-connected, too powerful to give even an inch."

Marc knew it. He hated that he did, but he understood. It was why he'd agreed to be a part of the operation, even after officially leaving the service. Not that he'd had much choice, but the undercover arms deals that the Chimère had facilitated had played a huge part in the ambush of his unit. Those illegal weapons had badly wounded several of the men he called brothers, then there was Cob...but he shut down that train of thought immediately. He would not think of Cob again, not on that day, anyway. He forced an image of his closest friend from before their first mission, two cocky bastards with shit-eating grins so certain of their own immortality, ready to protect and save the world. *That* was the Cob he wanted to remember.

"Understood," he confirmed in a tight voice.

"Good," Menzies returned. "I'll tell you what you're going to do. You get Target Alpha home and let her know that she had an unexpected allergic reaction, but she's fine now. Then you ask her brother to put you somewhere — *anywhere* — where she isn't. It's reported as rare, but sometimes, the memories of subjects did return with repeated exposure to the same individual."

The sick dread in the pit of Marc's stomach grew. "I won't lie to her directly about this...not if she remembers."

"I'm not asking you to...but we need to avoid that development if at all possible, and I think we both know that you aren't going to be able to just hand in your resignation." It was the first reference, oblique as it was, to the fact that Marc had essentially been forced into his role in the mission. "Isn't it better for her to think you're a horny asshole than for her to have to be put into the protective custody of Uncle Sam for however long it takes for all this to resolve?"

Marc couldn't imagine Clothilde — his sparkling, shimmering glow in a world of darkness — cooped up in a secret location somewhere, especially not now that she had finally started to come into her own. No matter how nice they made it, how beautifully they framed it, it would be a prison, and she'd had too many restrictions throughout her life to ever return to that.

"This is gonna suck ass, Menzies," he finally answered. The other man's answering laugh was humorless and sad.

"Always does, Constantin."

\* \* \* \*

It smelled like Marc. For one brief, shining moment, Clothilde felt a blissful excitement rise in her, sheer giddiness at the coming day. Then she opened her eyes and realized that, instead of waking up in the arms of the man she'd been dreaming of, even while she thought he despised her, she was instead lying in the same bed that had felt like her prison for months as she'd recovered from her car accident. Humming machines surrounded her, sleek and gleaming in the morning sunlight. Marc was there, but halfway across the room, almost entirely obscured by shadows. Still, she could tell he was frowning. No, *scowling* was a more apt description. *Did I imagine everything the night before?*

Her mind felt fuzzy, filled with a thick fog, but she remembered the softness of his lips, the tender way he'd touched her...his faintly spicy taste.

"Wh—" She cleared her throat on a croak. "What happened?" she whispered.

"There's water right next to you, if you turn your head." His voice was tight, nearly toneless.

She turned and was able to easily reach the long straw, sucking cold water, which felt like a balm to her ragged throat. Still, she stopped after two long pulls. She was no stranger to the rapid onset nausea that could happen when you drank too much.

"Better?" he rumbled, and something was...off about his voice, but she couldn't quite figure out what.

"Yeah," she whispered.

29

"You had an allergic reaction, a severe one."

Clothilde's mind raced. She had several food allergies, so she had to be extremely careful, but she didn't remember the usual itchiness, although she had certainly felt lightheaded when...they'd been kissing.

"We kissed?" she blurted out unthinkingly, and Marc gave a humorless laugh.

"That and more, and I'm so goddamn sorry I didn't realize you were...altered—not until it was almost too late." Marc was obviously trying to sound emotionless, but she could hear the self-loathing behind his words.

"It's—"

"No...don't try to sugarcoat it." Her heart clenched at the anguish she heard in his voice. "It was wrong, and I knew it. You almost died. But you got help just in time."

She took stock of her body, realizing that while she felt an all-over sense of exhaustion, she also still felt sort of buzzed. Oddly, her right side ached almost as much as her left. She assumed she must have been so oxygen deprived that they'd had to give her intravenous epinephrine.

"Did you tell my brothers?" she asked.

"No, sweetheart." Had his voice softened a little? "You asked me not to."

She heaved a sigh of relief. "Thank you." At least her brothers wouldn't come storming in here at any second...having to worry again about their emotional, weak little sister. She had determined never to be that sad, helpless young woman again.

Even in the early-morning shadows, she could see Marc's face twist with self-disgust. "It's the least I could do after mauling you...when you weren't yourself."

Clothilde remembered the wild passion, her frantic desperation for him to touch her. She felt her cheeks heat. "I, um, don't totally remember — or at least, it isn't very clear — but I think I was right there with you — "

"I can't let you try to make me feel better about this, Duchess." His voice was so harsh that she nearly flinched. "It was wrong and I knew it. It was one-hundred-percent my fault. Someone else is coming today to take over as your dedicated guard."

"*What*?" Clothilde gasped. She couldn't help it. Marc had been the first extra guard her oldest brother, Pierre, had hired after her car accident, and throughout her sometimes-grueling recovery, he'd always been a constant. He'd given her steady advice and encouragement, in spite of the dislike that she'd thought he'd felt for her. More, though, he'd been incredibly thorough at his job. She had felt safe, knowing that he was a professional. She'd trusted him before, and she still did.

He'd helped her when she was most vulnerable, watched her go from weak to strong, both physically and emotionally. She suddenly felt like everything she'd done over the past six months or longer — all the positive changes she'd made to herself since she'd finally admitted that she couldn't marry Claude, who had never truly cared about her — all that progress was erased. At the idea of Marc being gone, it was as if she were back to being the needy, immature, spoiled little rich girl her ex had always accused her of being. She hated it, but terror was like a living, breathing thing inside of her, a demon she faced every day. How hard would it be to face when the only man who helped keep the nightmares at bay was gone?

"I... Please don't leave." Her throat had gone so dry and tight that she had to force the words out on a whisper, but she knew Marc would still hear them. "I don't feel safe with anyone else," she confessed, ashamed of how true the words were, ashamed of her own weakness.

"I have to." Marc's words were thick with... *something*, and for a second, she thought he might change his mind, or at least explain. Instead, he went to the door with the eerily silent and graceful steps she'd come to associate with him. The latch was a soft snick in the silent room, but it sounded like a shot blast.

*"I don't feel safe with anyone else."* She had torn out his heart with her quiet words, so vulnerable, so trusting. He'd wanted nothing more than to tell her about his mission and Menzies, to just fuck off and go to her, put his arms around her and tell her that he'd never leave again. If this sting had just been about some low-level criminal, he would have done it. Hell, even if this had been about a high-level leak, he wouldn't have been able to stop himself. But goddamn it, this was about a wealthy, powerful gang of international criminals who had access to deeply classified information and were putting not only the safety of countless military personnel at stake but also innocent civilians. For whatever shitty reason, the universe had only seen fit to give them one clear lead. Clothilde's family was connected to the Chimère somehow, so he'd had to find the strength to walk away from the woman who represented everything he respected and cherished in this world.

His stomach churned and he actually felt hot bile rise in his throat as he forced his feet to move, one in front of the other, out of the front door of the Gaspard family seat—their compound, really. He'd known he shouldn't have even come—had been taking a big risk, even with staying in the shadows, but he hadn't been able to leave her without some sort of apology. As he slid behind the wheel of the massive, reinforced black SUV, he caught a glimpse of his face in the rearview mirror. He looked haggard, with haunted eyes. This was not the man he'd set out to become when he and Cob had signed up to be heroes.

His conversation with Pierre Gaspard, Clothilde's eldest brother and the head of the Gaspard family, had been a real shitshow, too. He'd had to do some fast talking, and he fucking hated lying to people he respected. As it was, Pierre had told him in no uncertain terms to stay the hell away from his sister, and Marc wasn't half-sure that Pierre didn't suspect some version of the truth.

Even still, he couldn't drive away without knowing that the agent he'd hand-picked to replace him as Clothilde's main guard was settled in. He waited, watching surreptitiously from his vehicle, until he saw another SUV pull up. The man who stepped out, Cain Foster, was an old friend and a helluva good soldier — a happily married soldier with a beautiful wife and three kids. The man shouldn't have been able to see him — shouldn't have known where he was — but Foster shot a jaunty salute in his specific direction.

Marc gave a reluctant grin. *Goddamn, Foster, always one step ahead*. Marc knew he'd get razzed mercilessly by his friend for calling in this favor, but for once, he didn't care. If he had to leave Clothilde, he would make sure she was as safe as she could be without him. Not for the first — or even the hundredth — time, he damned the Chimère to hell.

\* \* \* \*

After Marc left, shame and deep embarrassment rose inside Clothilde and the weight of her emotions pressed on her chest until she had to throw the sheet and soft blanket off herself. She, Clothilde Gaspard, who had made a solemn vow never to beg, plead or cringe for anyone again the way that she had for years for Claude, had now begged Marc Constantin three times in as many conversations—asking for his friendship the night before, pleading for his touch and revealing her desperation for him to stay.

She understood that he might think he was being noble about what had happened in the car, and she had certainly felt like she wasn't entirely acting like herself the night before, but she also hadn't done anything she hadn't wanted to do. Every touch, every kiss, every*thing*—she had dreamed of all that with him for months but never thought she would have the chance to act on those feelings. Of course, if things had gone further, she would have had to tell him her terrible secret—or maybe he'd already guessed. But no...how could he?

She might not remember the end of the evening clearly, but she remembered earlier, when she'd been very willing all on her own. Marc had seemed eager then, too—but more, he'd seemed sweet and kind and patient—nothing like the cold stranger who'd just left the room, the man who apparently found it easy to just walk away. No, it was more like he'd escaped. *Why am I not enough to make anyone want to stay?*

She swiped roughly at the tears that had managed to leak out of her eyes to roll down her cheeks. She sat up in bed more fully, satisfied when she only had a little more than the usual painful twinges in her muscles. For someone who had apparently almost died the night before, her body felt surprisingly okay.

As she thought again about Marc's words and departure, her shame grew into anger. No, the feeling went beyond anger into fury. *Who the hell is he to decide how I feel?* She'd had enough of that during her relationship with Claude.

She'd hidden it from her family, but almost from the beginning, Claude had tried to subtly cut her down and control her. It had seemed innocent at first, silly — a casual remark here and there. By the time she'd ended their engagement, he'd been keeping tabs on her constantly, virtually telling her what to do every minute of every day — and she'd let him. *She'd* let *him.* She'd let him hurt her in other ways...but she cut that thought off promptly. She didn't blame the young woman she'd been, and therapy had helped her understand why she'd acted the way she had, but she never wanted to feel that way again. She would never let *any* man or woman make her feel that way anymore.

She stiffened her spine and took another fortifying sip of cold water. She was Clothilde Gaspard, described somewhat regularly in fluffy magazine articles as one of the most beautiful women in the world. She was wealthy and powerful through her family, but she had also learned to be confident in her own intelligence. *Bon Dieu*, she could make *herself* feel safe. If her heart felt bruised, as if it had been kicked around a little bit, she could ignore that.

She picked up her cell phone, which someone — probably Marc again, *damn him* — had left within reaching distance on the nightstand.

When the line connected, her voice felt shaky. "*Âllo, Luc?*"

"*Clochette! J'adore toujours entendre ta voix, chérie, mais c'est bien trop tôt à Montréal, non? Est-ce que quelque' chose s'est passé?*"

She had always been closest to the youngest of her three older brothers, and Luc was uncannily accurate as he told her that he always loved to hear her voice but that it was too early in Montreal and asked if something had happened. She should have known he'd figure out something was up. It was already early afternoon in Paris, where he was. She sighed.

"Can we...not talk about it?" she answered with a question of her own.

Even though she'd chosen not to do a video call because she didn't want her brother to see her eyes, she could imagine the way his lips must have tightened with worry—and she could almost hear what was probably a brisk nod.

"*Bon, alors*...we won't speak of it." Clothilde felt a rush of gratitude and affection for Luc. If she'd called Pierre or Rémy, they would never have let her drop the subject...but Luc was different. He had his own secrets.

"Did you stun them last night with your charm and a new dress? But who am I kidding? Of course you did, *sirène*. I bet nobody even knew what hit them. Oh, and what did you think of Rémy's mysterious Annelise?" Luc's deliberately light tone made her want to cry, and she missed his face. All her brothers had taken turns keeping her company after her horrible break-up with Claude. Then, when she'd been so badly injured in the accident, they'd again made sure that one of them was always by her side.

Luc had spent the longest stretches with her, reverting from the serious, competitive businessman he'd become into the young boy he'd been growing up. He'd brought all her favorite comfort foods, played her videos of the silly heartthrobs she'd once loved before Claude had taken over. He'd even put on ridiculous puppet shows at the foot of her bed with the old—and frankly creepy—set of hand-puppets they'd nearly worn out when they'd been kids.

"*Lu-Louche*" — she used her childhood nickname for him — "can I..." Clothilde almost faltered. *Dieu*, she didn't know what she was going to do if he refused — if Luc didn't take her seriously. She took another calming breath, and it steadied her. "Are you still working with that arms instructor? *Monsieur Curaton*?"

"Ye-es." Luc's response was thoughtful, drawn-out.

"Do you...think he would take on another pupil?" she blurted in a rush.

She almost thought her brother wouldn't answer or that the call had dropped, but instead, he surprised her. "I'm sure of it. Do you want me to send the jet back to you or have one arranged sooner?"

Clothilde's eyes stung again, this time from gratitude at how lucky she was to have a brother who understood her. "Sooner would be perfect, *frèrot*."

# Chapter Three

"...Defendant has been remanded to military custody..." Clothilde knew that the judge was still speaking, because his lips were still moving, but she didn't hear anything else. The relief at his words was so intense that she staggered, grabbing onto the row of chairs in front of her, but one was wobbly, and she worried for an instant that she'd make a scene by fainting. In a typical courtroom, one person being unsteady might not have been so noticeable, but this was a closed session, with advance security clearance required. There were only three other people in the main seating area of the hushed, wood-paneled room, and the judge sat in front, joined by an inordinate amount of military security personnel who fanned out against the walls, so they would *definitely* notice if she collapsed.

Then Marc was there, wrapping one strong arm around her waist, and covering her other hand with his.

She should have known he'd notice her distress. She allowed herself to lean into his strength, just for an instant, before pulling away as she had done any time he'd touched her over the past twelve weeks that they'd been alone together in Boston. There'd been a moment—just one—right after he'd rescued her in Vermont, when she'd thought they'd reached an unspoken truce and everything was going to change, but it had passed, and they'd resumed their stilted interactions. Now, when she caught a glimpse of his expression through her eyelashes, he had the same stoic expression that he'd worn for the past nine months whenever she'd seen him…the expression that said he knew he deserved and expected her scorn. There was pain behind his eyes, though.

The judge had finished speaking, and several guards were leading Claude de Voltin away, the man she'd once thought she would marry and build a life with, the sweet little boy who had grown into a deranged adult man, hell-bent on destroying the Gaspard family. The revelation a few months ago that he'd been the mystery assailant behind the attacks on her family and his escape from custody and surprise direct assault of her and Marina Lopez only twelve weeks earlier still stunned her.

Claude was cuffed on both his wrists and his ankles, with thick chains between, so he couldn't move faster than a shuffle. He seemed oddly subdued, unlike the last time she'd seen him, when he'd beaten and tied her up along with Marina, Pierre's girlfriend and her future sister-in-law's best friend. Just as she had the thought of how calm Claude seemed, though, he lunged at her unexpectedly. The row in front of her prevented him from touching her, but he was so close she could see the mindless, wild hatred of her in his bloodshot blue eyes.

"You'll pay for testifying against me, *salope*." He sprayed spittle on her cheeks as he spoke, low and urgent. "It won't matter where I am. They're coming for you, to finish what I started—" He grunted as the guards pulled him backward. "You know something you shouldn't. I made sure I'll get what you owe me!" His speech cut off as they hurried him to the side door, and it closed behind him with a heavy *thunk*.

She took a tissue out of her sleek handbag and wiped the spit off her face, striving for calm, but she couldn't seem to prevent her fingers from trembling.

"Well, shit, sweetheart...sit down before you fall down, okay?" Marc gently pushed her into one of the flip-down padded chairs, a shocking color of burnt orange that clashed with everything else in the room. She barely felt his hand, though, as his words rang in her ear. He hadn't called her sweetheart since the morning he'd left after the night in the sedan, so long ago now. Escaping from where she'd forced it to remain buried, she had a sharp memory of how amazing she'd felt in his arms, followed by a flash of something else...something unexpected. A hospital? With people in military uniforms all around her? *Que diable*?

She looked up in time to see one of the military guards who had been standing at the edges of the room give a significant look to Marc. The other man was tall and burly, so fit that his muscles probably had muscles underneath his neat uniform. Marc stiffened almost imperceptibly.

"Wait here a minute for me?" It sounded like a question, but it was really a statement, as Marc was already headed across the room to the man. They slipped into a side-vestibule room together.

"Did de Voltin just say that Target Alpha knew something she shouldn't?" Menzies's face was impassive and his lips barely moved, but the excitement in his voice was unmistakable.

"Yeah, he did," Marc confirmed, wishing he could have kept it to himself. His own radar had started pinging like crazy at that comment, and as a soldier and operative, he recognized that it could be just the break they'd been waiting for. As a man, though, rage and worry had coursed through him like a wildfire.

"She still hasn't remembered the military hospital or the *RK781*, correct?" His superior's voice was so low that Marc had to strain his ears to hear it, even as close as he stood in the empty room.

"Affirmative. As I told you, it was…unavoidable for us to go together to Vermont and to keep close to de Voltin to ensure he remained in custody this time. She hasn't shown a glimmer of recollection." Dryly, Marc reflected that she'd shown him anger, disappointment and open disdain, but she certainly hadn't acted like she remembered more than she should. Once or twice, he'd dared to hope she might be able to forgive him…but then the mask of indifference had returned. In any case, he didn't deserve her forgiveness.

Menzies's nod was small and clipped. "Seems unlikely at this point, then." He paused for just an instant. "New plan, Constantin. Don't lock her up, but stay with her twenty-four seven. Try to figure out what she knows. It must be something she's unaware of. No getting too close, though." Menzies coughed and actually looked uncomfortable for a moment.

Marc bristled.

"That directive's not from me. We're getting pressure on this, and if you look too friendly, or there's even a breath of it, we're out." His face was stony. Yep, Menzies was pissed off.

Marc digested the older man's statement, trying to read between the lines. Someone was pulling some very lofty strings and had some brass balls indeed to get that sort of reaction from Menzies. His CO had put in a lot of his own time and energy on this op, too. It had even cost him his wife, who had walked out on him a few months earlier, if the rumor mill was to be believed.

The man continued. "With de Voltin's connections, someone is going to make a move on her, probably sooner rather than later. Be prepared."

Marc stiffened, shooting his focus to Menzies' face. The older man had a thick scar running from his ear down to his neck, snaking like an angry red river. It looked like someone had tried to hack Menzies' head off, and right now, Marc could understand the sentiment.

"I'm not using her as bait." His voice was low and scary, even to his own ears.

"For fuck's sake, I'm not asking you to. Most of the men in our unit are half in love with her, and the rest of 'em are all the way there. I'd have a goddamn mutiny." He stepped closer, his huge frame towering over even Marc's. "We both know there's no place she can go to be safe, not with the Chimère's connections. It's only a question of when she'll next be attacked, so I'm just asking—no, I'm *ordering*—you to be ready."

Marc's jaw was so tight that he was surprised his teeth didn't splinter. He hated that he recognized the truth in Menzies's words.

"Fine. I want Clark and Barnes back on Clothilde's detail, though."

Menzies raised one eyebrow at this request, a large show of restraint for him.

"She...*likes* them." Marc answered the unspoken question gruffly. Clark, in particular, made her smile...in a way he never had.

"Done," Menzies agreed, and Marc was dismissed.

\* \* \* \*

"If I ask you who that man was — the man in uniform you slipped away with — is there any chance that you'll tell me?" Clothilde tried to keep her voice casual as she spoke to Marc from the backseat of the car. It was ridiculous, since there were only the two of them and he wasn't really a driver anyway, but since Serge had been on an extended medical leave for the past nine months, Marc had insisted on driving. He also insisted on her sitting in the back because he said it offered better protection. Clothilde thought it was just another way for him to put distance between them — emotional and literal.

Marc looked at her in the rearview mirror, but she couldn't see his blue eyes, which were shadowed. "Sure. He's an old friend."

Clothilde pursed her lips. "If you're going to lie, then just don't answer."

There was a long silence.

"I'm sorry. Did you think that after being raised with three brothers, then spending years as an accessory to a megalomaniac controlling asshole, I never learned how to read body language?" Clothilde's tone was sharper than she'd intended. She had vowed not to let Marc see how deeply he'd affected her all those months ago, but she was tired. The look in Claude's eyes had shaken her up. He'd looked insane. Not even a shadow of the young man she'd once cared for had lurked behind his wild, accusing stare. More, it had made some of her worst memories rise to the surface again, so that her very skin felt tender.

"Fine," Marc acknowledged, "I won't answer."

The satisfaction that she felt at winning was hollow. Traffic was heavy in downtown Boston — stop-and-go traffic as opposed to the usual slow crawl — so it took her a couple of minutes to realize that he was heading toward the skyscraper where she was currently keeping a palatial apartment. Well, technically she supposed it was Rémy's, but he never spent the night anywhere other than Annelise's place when they were in town, so it had seemed silly for her to get something else.

"Oh, take the left here instead. You can just drop me off on Newbury Street. I texted Annelise, and I'm meeting her for coffee and something sweet." Now she had his full attention. He tried to catch her gaze in the rearview mirror, but she avoided it. "I guess this is probably goodbye, right? Since now —" Her voice hitched in spite of her best efforts to sound casual. She took a steadying breath. "Now Claude is truly in custody, where he'll hopefully stay. I'm sure you want to go back to…whatever you were doing…like you did before. You'll send Cain Foster back instead." She made a waving motion but snatched her hand back to her chest when she realized it had a slight tremor.

The past weeks with Marc, from the moment she'd insisted on coming with him to Vermont where Pierre had been trapped in their cabin with Marina and attacked by Claude, had been sweet agony. In spite of her anger — and *bon Dieu*, she was furious — nobody else made her feel like Marc did. She wanted to hate him, had *tried* to hate him, but her resolve had nearly cracked when he'd almost been killed by Claude as Marc had leaped to save Marina's life. She'd had to rebuild it, piece by piece, preparing for this moment—the moment that Marc would surely leave her again.

After all, it wasn't as if he wanted to be near her. He had never *wanted* to be with her at all—had never chosen it. He was a paid bodyguard—an amazing one—but this was his job. *She* was a job…and one he was probably just counting down the days until he could give two weeks' notice to. She was happy to save him the trouble.

"Do you really think it's a good idea? Knowing that there is an unknown partner out there, according to Claude—especially after that scene in the courtroom? You would be awfully exposed, out in public." Marc sounded reasonable, and she must have been imagining it, but he also sounded genuinely concerned. Clothilde couldn't stand it for another second, the pretense of caring.

"Empty threats. Claude's in secure custody now, right? So why shouldn't I? Unless there's something you haven't told me?" His silence was the only response, thick and heavy in the confined space. Frustration and hurt rose in her chest.

The car stopped again, having only moved a couple car-lengths since she'd asked Marc to turn left. Without thinking too deeply, she scooted over and opened the door.

"This is taking too long. I'll just walk." She congratulated herself on the brightness of her voice, which was almost convincing, then she was free in the warm summer sunlight. She felt a secret satisfaction in Marc's loud curse as he hit the steering wheel, unable to move forward or pull over on the narrow, crowded street.

# Chapter Four

"I don't think I've ever seen Marc look quite so surly," Annelise commented, and Clothilde darted a glance over at Marc, who was folded uncomfortably onto one of the antique-looking pink velvet chairs. "And that's saying something," her future sister-in-law added wryly.

Clothilde narrowed her eyes. By the time he had found a place for the car — and she honestly wasn't sure what he'd done with it — and hurried after her, she and Annelise had already been settled into a sumptuous corner booth with coffee. He'd been staring daggers at her ever since he'd stalked in.

"He is kind of like a… What's the word?" Clothilde searched her mind for the English word to match the image of a *corbeau*. "Ah, yes, *corbeau* is raven, *non*? Like a giant, grim raven, always hovering close by." She paused, knowing she was being unfair. "Although I may have, uh, jumped out and left him in the car while it was still technically moving."

"You didn't!" Annelise's eyes widened, then sparkled with mirth. "But of course you did. Marc must have had steam coming out of his ears."

Clothilde took a sip of her coffee. It was strong and hot with a lot of milk, just the way she liked it. "I think I learned some new words... He does have a tendency to use colorful language."

Annelise snorted. "Only around you, Clo. The rest of us are lucky to hear two words from him. When he saved my life and Rémy's, he barely batted an eyelash."

Clothilde had liked Annelise from the moment Rémy had first introduced them, and in the past months, the two women had become fast friends. Her brother's fiancée was beautiful, smart, funny and madly in love with Rémy — so deeply that it sometimes roused uncomfortable prickles of envy in Clothilde — which was horrible, since why wouldn't she want the best for her sweetest brother? Annelise was certainly the best — with the only possible exception of her closest friend, Marina, who had recently gotten together with Pierre. It was only that surrounded by so much love, it was all the more lonely for Clothilde on her own.

She didn't realize the silence had stretched so long until Annelise leaned over, her faint vanilla-spice scent like a delicious hug.

"You seem like you maybe don't want to talk about it...but did something happen between the two of you? That first night I met you at that event in Montreal — holy guacamole, you could have cut the sexual tension between you and Marc with a steak knife — but then, you barely spoke for months, hardly saw each other. You still seem...strained."

As it had so many times since that night, Clothilde's mind went back to the taste of Marc's drugging kisses, the intensity of the pleasure from his hands, his mouth. Pathetic, but it had been the best sexual experience of her life—even after two years engaged to Claude… *especially* after two years engaged to that monster. Something flitted again at the edge of her consciousness…something she needed to remember.

"It's…complicated," she hedged, trying to be vague, although apparently not vague enough.

"I *knew* it!" Annelise proclaimed, then lowered her voice to just above a whisper again. "I haven't told Rémy, because obviously he would go absolutely crazy if he even suspected anything, since you're his baby sister…but there's something about the way that man looks at you—"

"Like I'm dog puke on the sidewalk?" Clothilde suggested.

Annelise rolled her eyes. "No…not at all. Oh, Marc obviously wants to seem like he doesn't care…but, Clo, when nobody is looking, he stares at you with these hungry eyes…like he's been stranded on a desert island and you're the only glass of water." She took a long sip of her own coffee and raised her eyebrows significantly.

"I think you're imagining that," Clothilde answered, but deep in her gut, stubborn hope fluttered painfully back to life.

Annelise glanced at Marc again, so far across the room that he couldn't possibly hear their words over the general din and conversation of the café. Clothilde thought that her friend was probably trying to be surreptitious, but she only managed to be obviously furtive, and Marc drew his dark blond eyebrows together farther, deepening his scowl. Annelise scooted closer to Clothilde in the booth, so they were practically touching sides. Clothilde wanted to laugh.

"Don't you think there's something...*hinky* about his background?" Annelise breathed the question.

Clothilde opened her mouth to deny it, but then...she wasn't so sure. "He certainly has had some serious training. I mean, I couldn't believe how he and Barnes just went after Claude with some crazy moves...but I know he's some sort of an American military hero who retired and went into security, so that makes more sense. A lot of retired military go into those types of jobs."

"On paper, it makes sense," Annelise agreed. "But the crazy extra security around Brian Clark when he was in the hospital...then the way that Pierre hasn't fired Marc, even though he forbade him from making a move on you or even getting too close to you—"

"Pierre did *what*?" The question was sharper and louder than Clothilde had intended, and a couple of the other café patrons looked over. Marc made a move as if to get up, so Clothilde aimed a vague, reassuring smile in the general direction of the room. She lowered her voice. "My overbearing, pompous oaf of a brother did *what*?"

"I thought you knew... Marina told me. I guess there's some sort of tense understanding between Pierre and Marc that he's supposed to stay away from you. But, *obviously*, that hasn't exactly been happening."

At Annelise's words, righteous anger rose like a wild thing in Clothilde's chest. *Was the understanding with Pierre the reason Marc left?* The reason that, even over the past few weeks where she'd seen Marc nearly every day to deal with something related to Claude, he still wouldn't get too close to her? *Mais non*, Marc wasn't a man to be dissuaded from anything he really wanted, no matter what. She knew that much about him. Still, she was beyond furious with her *conard* of an oldest brother. *How did he dare!* Marc should have told her, too.

"Uh oh, your eyes are flashing…like, I think I can see sparks practically shooting out of them." Annelise's words were teasing, but there was real concern on her face.

Clothilde took a deep breath. "No… I mean, sure, I'm maybe a little bit…massively offended, but I've gotten over worse." She was still seething, but she pushed it down. This wasn't the time or the place, and she wasn't kidding that she'd had a ton of practice at continuing to act like everything was light and fun when in fact it was the opposite. It was time for some redirection.

"You said there was a reason you chose this café, right? I love the décor." Looking around, Clothilde realized that it was true. There was a classic Art Deco feel, with bright and bold colors, but with softer hints of romantic and feminine fabrics and colors.

Annelise still looked worried, but as Clothilde had expected, her brother's fiancée was too kind not to go along with the change in subject. "It *is* pretty, isn't it? Yeah, this place and the bakery next door are owned by the same woman…and I've heard amazing things about her desserts, so I wanted to scope it out to see if we should consider asking her to help with the wedding. I, um, don't think she does weddings, but I thought she might…"

"Agree for the famous Gaspards?" Clothilde's smile widened into an authentic one. "It's a good thought."

Annelise's cheeks grew rosy. "I mean, it's not like I would force her or anything. It's just that Rémy and I want something different, and most of the 'wedding bakeries' are so stodgy. Well, really, *I* want something non-traditional, and Rémy just tells me that whatever makes me happy will make him happy." Annelise trailed off, her eyes soft and dreamy. "He's so amazing, sweet, *sexy*..."

"Hey! *Ah-ah!*" Clothilde held up a hand laughingly. "Please stop there! You're talking about *mon frère!*"

"I mean, you kind of just have to deal with the fact that your brother is like Prince Charming if he were built like a—"

"Oh, *Dieu merci!* The food is here!" Clothilde interrupted Annelise, who burst out laughing.

Eyeing the multiple trays, heavy with a multitude of fancy, sweet confections, Clothilde raised an eyebrow and gave Annelise a speaking glance. "And that is a *lot* of food."

Annelise shrugged sheepishly. "I wanted to order one of everything that looked good...and I'm pretty hungry."

"I skipped breakfast and haven't had lunch yet," Clothilde answered. She'd been so nervous for the hearing that morning that the thought of food had turned her stomach. Marc had chided her for not taking care of herself. She shook off the memory. "I'm up for at least a bite of everything, for sampling purposes."

The bright shine of Annelise's smile practically lit up their side of the room. "Perfect!"

* * * *

Clothilde had been cool to him all afternoon—no, not just cool, ice cold. He had no way to confirm it, other than having read his name on their lips a couple times at the café, but he suspected it had to do with something Annelise had told her. She'd ignored him as if she didn't even know him as they'd walked back to the car on Newbury Street, and while she hadn't protested as he'd accompanied her in the private express elevator to the forty-ninth floor of the skyscraper where the ultramodern apartment was, her complete silence was almost worse than her usual barbs.

After informing him that they were still also going to a fundraiser gala with Rémy and Annelise that night and not waiting for his reply, she'd disappeared into her bedroom and bathroom suite to prepare. That had been two hours ago, though, and now he was getting pissed off. The stunt she'd pulled earlier, jumping out of a moving car to saunter down the street, unprotected, while he'd paid the valet of a nearby restaurant an exorbitant amount of money to take the car and look the other way, had been reckless. *No, damn it.* It had been idiotic—and damned dangerous. It was also unlike her. Clothilde could be stubborn...but usually wasn't at the expense of reason.

Not knowing how long she'd be, he'd long since made the quick switch into the suit he kept in the front closet. If he were a real party guest, he would have needed a tuxedo, but a suit was okay for the hired help...*the brainless muscle.* He tried to shrug off his negative thoughts—what the hell did he care if a bunch of rich people who loved to hear their own voices thought he was beneath them?—but it wasn't working, and he knew why. Clothilde had never looked at him before today with such open animosity in her eyes. Disappointment, hurt, betrayal...sure, but something about her expression as she'd announced, defiantly, that they were going to the gala tonight had made him feel less-than. God, he was used to being treated that way, had been from the earliest time he could remember, but never from *her*.

He'd thought about her every day, every minute, every *fucking second* since he'd left. He'd called and texted for updates until Foster had become genuinely concerned, and even then, he hadn't been able to stop himself. Foster had been obviously relieved to get away from the situation when his wife went into labor with their fourth baby.

When Marc had seen Clothilde again, it had been the sweetest kind of torture until he'd almost lost her. He'd aged ten years in the hours that Claude had held Clothilde and Marina captive. Through it all, he'd known that while they couldn't be anything more to each other, at least they still had *something*...their connection, whatever it was. Because of his orders, he'd tried to sever it, but he'd still *seen* it in her eyes, and he'd held on to it like a lifeline.

Now, though, something had changed, and it was making his heart hurt. He tugged irritably at his collar, his tie feeling suddenly too tight. What the hell was she thinking, going to a gala where a crowd of people, some of them unknowns, would be? One of the guests would almost certainly be the Chimère, who had to be a member of her social circle. He knew that this was almost exactly the opportunity that Menzies was looking for and that he'd agreed to, but he didn't like it like this.

This felt too much like actually using Clothilde as bait, without her knowledge or consent. He'd made several calls to set up extra details for the party, but she didn't know that...and it felt wrong. His gut was blaring a warning at him. It was foolish, after Claude's comments, not to exercise at least some level of caution, but she was diving headlong into danger...for what? She didn't need free champagne... She could buy a bar today with cash — or a whole vineyard, if she wanted. Was it the attention? Was the admiration of her peers really so important that she would potentially risk her life for it? *Fuck that.*

He stood and pushed open the doors to her bathroom and changing room suite, and his temper heated even further when he saw that she just stood in the middle of the spacious changing area, still in a silky purple robe, clutching a thick, diamond necklace.

"It's been two hours and you haven't even chosen a dress?" He knew he sounded like a dick, but he couldn't seem to stop it. "Are you really so afraid of an argument with me over your idiotic idea to go to this party — or are you just that vain?"

"How dare you barge into my private space and speak to me that way!" Her cheeks flushed and her deep breaths made the fabric over them shine with the movement. Clothilde in her anger was magnificent, but he wouldn't be deterred.

"I dare because you left me waiting on you for over two hours, Duchess, after decreeing to the commonfolk that we were going to a gala instead of keeping a low profile. Do you really crave male attention so much that you'd risk your life for it? You can't skip a single event or they won't write you up in all of those glossy French magazines? Is that it?"

"Is that really what you think of me?" Her eyes practically glowed with anger, like two hot coals.

"What else can I think? It was bad enough when you ran off like a child this afternoon, but now, you won't even consider crying off tonight? Didn't you understand what de Voltin said to you?"

The necklace trembled in her hand, but she raised her chin defiantly, and he noticed for the first time that her eyes were red-rimmed with faint traces leading down her cheeks, as if she'd been crying. His heart squeezed in his chest.

"I understood him. Do you think that's the first time he has threatened me?" Her voice was quiet but steely.

An ugly suspicion took root in Marc's gut. "He threatened you when you were together?"

She looked away, and the thick silence was a palpable thing. "He gave me this necklace, you know? When we were first engaged and he still acted like he... I'd forgotten I'd even left it in my travel jewelry case."

Marc stayed silent, all his anger seeping away. "I'm sorry, sweetheart."

Her eyes looked shiny before she turned away again. "That's over now." Her voice wobbled a little, but she sounded determined. "If I stayed at home every time someone told me they wanted to kill me or wanted me to die, I'd never leave my bedroom."

She was obviously trying for a light tone but it fell flat, and Marc's blood ran cold.

"What do you mean?" He was afraid he already had an idea.

"When all those glossy magazines and social websites write articles about me, the response is always mixed. Lots of people are just lovely—especially when I was recovering from my accident—but some of them are pretty negative."

"How negative?" He tried to keep the scary note out of his voice, and he must have succeeded, probably because she still wasn't looking at his face.

Her laugh was humorless, sad. "Well, let's put it this way...my manager, Clément, prints them out, you know, just in case."

Marc nodded. "Old-school back-up."

"They used to fit in one file cabinet drawer, then the whole cabinet, and now I think his assistant has a whole filing room."

A cold knot of stone settled in his gut. If he hadn't known her better, hadn't spent months observing the nuances of her expressions, the brave façade that she put up for everyone in her life, he would have believed that she was unconcerned...flippant, even. But Marc knew her—knew her better than she probably wanted anyone to—and he could see that it hurt her.

"Doesn't Clément call the police?" His voice was low, dangerous...accusatory.

She shrugged, the creamy slopes of her bosom glowing in the V of skin exposed by her robe. "He used to call pretty often—and Villiers, as well." Villiers was the long-time head of security at her family's estate. "Now I think he only calls them for the really detailed ones—you know, more inside info than someone should know, credible-sounding death threats?"

Marc felt frozen to the spot. He knew her background—knew she was the famous only daughter of an absurdly wealthy and powerful family, knew she had put herself into the public eye as a model and had become a popular celebrity—and he'd thought he understood the threats to her, but he'd apparently only seen the tip of the iceberg.

Clothilde continued before he could formulate a response that wouldn't horrify her. "So you see, Claude's threats aren't my first this month — probably not even my first this week."

"What. The. *Hell*." He knew he was growling, but his body went hot, then cold, then hot again. How had he not been aware of this before? *You never asked her*, a small voice whispered in his head.

Clothilde held herself stiff, as though expecting his censure, and Marc realized that she did that a lot — not usually around him as much, but around almost everyone else. Around her brothers, even, and he knew how much she cherished them.

"It's none of your business. I don't know why I even mentioned it, except that I refuse to be held captive by threats — threats from a known liar in supposedly ultra-secure US government custody, I might add — when these types of comments are a part of my daily life. They have been since I was a child."

Marc knew that she'd been trained from a young age to defend herself. There had been several kidnapping attempts on all the Gaspard children. Somehow, though, he hadn't thought about what form that interest would evolve into as she became an adult. The Chimère was more than just some greedy amateur wanting to ransom her, though. Not for the first time, he wished like hell that he could ignore his orders and tell her everything. He'd been able to tell Pierre a little more, in confidence, because of the man's background assistance on several Canadian military projects, but Menzies had been crystal clear that Clothilde and her other two brothers were not to have more information, for fear of compromising the investigation.

"If we're done, please leave so I can finish getting dressed." Clothilde's voice had turned imperious and cold, so that the mask was back in place. She was likely trying to protect herself with the mental distance, but he wasn't sure he gave a shit anymore, not when her safety was concerned.

"Like hell, Duchess. You can pretend that nothing bothers you and that you don't care, but I know you do. Going to this party tonight is foolish…reckless. And if I have to pick you up, put you over my knee and spank that luscious little ass of yours until you can't sit for a week, I will do it."

The image he described made his cock, always hard around her, thicken even further so that he was surprised he didn't pop open the zipper of his cheap suit pants. He had a momentary hesitation when he thought he'd gone too far, but even though her cheeks pinkened and her eyes flashed, he could tell by how fast she was breathing that the idea aroused as much as it angered her.

"You don't have the right to speak to me that way, Marc. You gave it up when you left me alone after my allergic reaction nine months ago." Her eyes were fathomless. "When you apparently promised my brother you'd stay away from me."

Her soft words, filled with a world of hurt and betrayal, were like a punch to the gut…with brass knuckles. She was right. The rage drained out of him, leaving only deep concern. Even though she wasn't entirely correct, it didn't change the way things had to be between them.

"I wish…so badly…that things were different, sweetheart." He wanted to say more but knew that he couldn't. He cleared his throat. "But no matter what else has happened, I hope you know I want to protect you."

The fire seemed to have gone out of her, too, leaving her looking sad and drawn. "Yes, I know it must be part of what made you such a wonderful soldier. You care deeply about your job."

Without thinking, he took the few steps across plush carpet of the dressing room to reach her, and he put his hand on her shoulder. Even through the thin fabric of her robe, he felt the heat of her skin and the faint tremble.

"You have to know you aren't just a job to me." The words were raspy, forced out of his throat. *Goddamn Menzies for putting me in this position.* His superior would probably be happy to have Clothilde go to parties, cafés, anywhere...as long as it drew out the Chimère. He had to obey orders, but he didn't have to go along with them blindly. Clothilde was *his* woman, his to protect and care for, no matter how she felt about him.

"Do I?" she shot back, looking pointedly at his hand. He reluctantly took it away.

"Be mad at me, Duchess. Furious. I just want you be alive and unharmed while you do it."

Her gaze shot to his as the honesty she must have heard in his voice. He meant every goddamn word, like an oath. *Please, God, let this woman live and be happy...even if it's without me.*

She sighed, the motion making the low light ripple and gleam off the soft fabric draped around her.

"I suppose I shouldn't have jumped out of the car on Newbury Street...and I didn't absolutely need to meet Annelise, at least not that way. I just— I had to feel free.

What does it matter if Claude is locked up if I'm still a prisoner?"

Marc considered her words. "I get that. I'm not trying to make you feel like a prisoner. It's just...still dangerous."

The spark of understanding lit her eyes. "I see."

He was afraid that she did see, too much. "So, you know why it would be idiotic to go tonight?"

"Can you tell me exactly why I should be worried?" Her question was veering into dangerous territory.

"No, I can't tell you that," he answered, knowing that he was walking a dangerous line.

"Can't...or won't?" she prodded.

*Ah, shit.* "Both," he answered, knowing it wasn't what she wanted to hear.

The rich chocolate-brown of her eyes grew shadowed, and she stiffened her shoulders. The movement made her drop the necklace she was still clutching. He bent to retrieve it, intending to put it back into her outstretched hand, but instead, he dropped it on the table and took her hand into his.

"Baby, you're bleeding," he exclaimed, ignoring the spark of awareness that flashed through him at the contact of her bare skin against his. As he studied her hand, he saw that the thick jewelry, which must have been worth a fortune, had scored slices into her soft palm. There were angry red indents where it hadn't cut her. How hard had she been holding it?

"It's nothing." She tried to take her hand back, but he held firm. "Just need to wash it with some soap."

"It's not nothing, Duchess. Some of these cuts look pretty deep." He stroked his finger gently over the base of her thumb, tenderly, and he felt an answering quiver of awareness go through her frame. "You said de Voltin gave this to you, but there's more."

He made the statement a question, and she bit her lip. Something in her expression made a dark suspicion rise in his throat, and he felt as if he might be sick. Still, he wanted to hear it from her — to understand.

"Sammy's Spot, the charity shelter that we're fundraising for tonight is a good one... *the best*. And I'm on the board of trustees, although our names aren't public."

"Oka-ay." He wondered at the change of subject, when he'd thought she would say something more about the necklace. He continued stroking small circles over the uninjured parts of her palm, even though he knew he should stop, mesmerized by the silky softness of her skin...her warmth. "Even fundraising for Mother Theresa isn't worth your life, is it?"

The sadness and horror that he saw in her eyes gutted him. "I might just owe them my life, Marc." The pieces clicked together with a terrible clarity, and he kicked himself for being such an idiot. He'd seen all the signs before — dammit, he'd *lived* them when he'd been a kid. He'd just assumed that she had been protected by her family's wealth and power, but he should have known better.

"Oh, sweetheart," he started, but she stopped him with a furious glare. He didn't think he'd ever seen anyone so beautiful as she was when she was angry.

"No...don't you *dare* pity me. And don't tell my family, either. They just think that it's another one of my pet projects — nothing special. If they knew the truth, it would hurt them so much." She took a shaky breath. "But now you see, I have to go tonight to bring more attention, more funding. I donate extremely generously but there's always more to be done, more women and children to help. Starting a new life can be so dangerous and expensive. Funding from more wealthy donors, even if they only show up because they want to meet me and Rémy and Annelise, could make all the difference to so many families."

He ached for her…physically ached for the trauma she must have been through. And how had her family not noticed? But then again, how the hell had he never guessed, either?

"All right. Let's put together a plan so you stay safe, though. I'm not going to stay on the sidelines like I usually do." He could tell he'd surprised her with his easy agreement, but how could he argue against something that was obviously so important to her.

"That's it? You're just…*agreeing*?" Her expression was dubious.

Marc gave a short nod. "I still don't like it. In fact, I think I'm going to hate every fucking minute until I have you locked back up again behind some very thick doors, just like I hated worrying about every single person that walked by the café this afternoon when you and Annelise were just sitting there, eating cream puffs like sitting ducks—but I get it now. Thank you for trusting me, baby."

He raised her palm to his face and placed a soft kiss right in the middle, making her exhale in a soft gasp. He'd thought that he couldn't be more enchanted by her, with her stunning beauty, kindness, quick humor and quiet determination, but he'd been so wrong. She had faced darkness head-on, time and again, and still had a backbone of steel. He was in such deep shit, but he didn't even want a shovel.

"Okay, then," she answered in a breathy voice, and he could actually see her bringing the mask of haughty superiority down again onto her features, but he knew that was all it was—a disguise. No, it was more than a disguise... It was *armor*.

He turned to leave. "Oh, and, sweetheart, I feel a lot of things for you, but none of them is pity." He should have left it at that. He was so close to the door, but an imp—or maybe even a demon—urged him on. "Let me know if you need help zipping up your dress, hm-m?"

# Chapter Five

*Lighter.* She hadn't been certain earlier, but now she realized that was the sensation she'd been feeling as she'd finished getting ready and during the short car ride over...so much lighter, like she'd lost fifty pounds of pure guilt. And *fils de putain*, wasn't that just messed up? It wasn't as if Marc was the only person who knew — although he was the only friend she'd come out and told. Was he even her friend? Employee? More? Nothing? She hadn't even told him the whole story, and she wasn't sure if she would. She wanted to, since she knew it could have been so much worse for her — *was* so much worse for many of the women and children she was devoted to helping — but he'd understood anyway. *If he understood how you feel*, a little voice whispered in the back of her mind, *then he knew how much he hurt you when he left.*

She was distracted from her own dismal thoughts as they pulled to a slow stop in the circular driveway in front of the Bostonian Aquarium. She was the one who had suggested the location—people loved events that had a bit of a twist—and she'd been grateful they'd been able to rent out the entire place and get permission to bring in outside caterers, staff, lighting engineers and a string quartet who had promised to play quietly in deference to the fish and other aquatic creatures.

It had come at a price, but Clothilde was happy to be donating funds for some of the excellent marine conservation programs through the aquarium, and the support and influence of some of the attendees who were expected would be worth it. Annelise had even invited two judges, along with an Assistant District Attorney. It was astonishing the number of people her future sister-in-law had met through her job as an event coordinator for a financial company, and Annelise's boss and mentor, Charles Pinkston, had been delighted to lend his support and contact list.

Frankly, after Charles had been deceived and kidnapped by Claude because of his business connections to her family, Clothilde was grateful—and surprised—that Charles was even still on speaking terms with them, but he'd been extremely gracious about the incident. Of course, the fact that he treated Annelise like a second daughter probably had something to do with it. Even in the dim twilight, Clothilde thought she caught a glimpse of his familiar, elegant figure in the main entrance.

She saw Marc slip the valet something before he instructed tersely, "Put it out front...as close as you can."

The young valet bobbed his head, pocketing the bills and sprinting off, and she wondered exactly how much Marc had tipped. Then he came around to help her out of the car and she forgot every other thought as his warm, rough hand connected with the bare skin exposed by the low-cut back of her dress. It was a relatively warm night, a true midsummer evening, and under the thick smells of the city, there was a freshness, like grass and rain and flowers, probably from the gardens in the nearby parks. There was a stiff breeze, though, this close to the water, and the air held an unmistakable salty tang. Goosebumps rose on her back and chest, and Marc leaned closer, as if he would shelter her from the wind.

"Cold, Duchess?" His gravelly voice in her ear made her shiver, but from awareness instead of from the cool air.

"Just a little," she acknowledged, surprising them both. She normally kept quiet, pushed through, did what was needed...but something had changed between them in her dressing room. She wasn't sure yet exactly what it was, and it probably wasn't even safe for her to know. Marc slid his hand as if to wrap his arm around her, but he froze in the middle of the gesture, as though he'd remembered just in time that he wasn't supposed to touch her.

It shouldn't have, but it hurt her. *He can't even touch me now?* She deftly sidled away from him and hurried ahead to the entrance before he could say anything — if he'd even been planning to say something.

She'd been correct in recognizing Charles Pinkston, who stood with both Annelise and her brother Rémy near the entrance. Charles was the first to greet her, kissing the back of her hand. He looked charming and urbane, and the smile he flashed at her was warm and friendly, but not for the first time, she thought he still looked sad.

"So lovely to see you, Charles! It's been too long," she enthused, only remembering after he raised one sardonic eyebrow that she'd seen him at dinner at Annelise's apartment only days earlier.

"*Indeed*," he agreed, but his eyes gleamed. "You look lovely, as always, Clothilde."

Annelise hugged her then kissed her on each cheek in the hybrid French-Canadian-American greeting that she'd adopted with the Gaspard family. "He's right, Clo. You look ravishing, and you smell amazing, too. You're like a designer mermaid." She paused and sniffed appreciatively. "And whatever that scent is, it's divine."

Clothilde was torn between amusement and affection. "I think it's just my perfume, from Grasse," she said, smiling. It was a scent that she'd had custom-made directly by one of the big perfumiers, working with a consultant directly to assess the fragrance notes that would complement her natural chemistry the best. "We should take a trip to Nice and Cannes together soon... I think Luc's planning to be down there in a couple of weeks. That is, if Rémy can stand to be away from you for a few days?"

Her second-oldest brother enveloped her in a hug before kissing her on both cheeks, and for some reason, her eyes began to feel suspiciously watery.

"*Clochette*?" he asked questioningly, searching her face, but she gave a stiff nod that was more of just an incline of her head. Wise brother, he backed off, and his expression of concern melted into his usual easy warmth.

"I agree with Charles and Annelise, *chérie*. You look beautiful tonight, like your dress was made for this party."

Looking down, Clothilde realized that her brother's comment was true. The beading on her silvery-blue dress caught in the low blue lighting of all the tanks that surrounded them, making her shine like a pearl. "Thanks," she answered, feeling another swell of emotion as she looked at the three of them. She was incredibly lucky to have such an amazing family and friends, but she also felt so alone.

"As for stealing my fiancée... Don't you think it would be more fun if I came along instead?" The look of absolute love and devotion Rémy gave to Annelise made Clothilde's heart squeeze in her chest. Her brother leaned down to whisper something for Annelise's ears only, but Clothilde caught something that sounded suspiciously like, "*like to thoroughly explore the smooth rock beaches with my sea goddess.*" Whatever he'd said, it made Annelise flush a bright pink.

Marc's warm bulk behind her surprised her, but it shouldn't have. They'd agreed at the apartment that he needed to stay closer to her than usual, ready for whatever might come. Instead of remaining on the fringes and in his usual dark suit, he'd coordinated with the concierge of her building to have a tux delivered.

Rémy and Charles's faces registered mild surprise, but Annelise's reflected interested speculation.

Her brother was the first to recover. "Constantin. Nice to see you. I know you and Clochette have been tied up with all the legal red tape, but I heard the good news about Claude this morning from Pierre."

*Bon Dieu*, Rémy was really good at this smooth talking, no matter how much he hated these types of events. Marc had been all but avoiding her and her

Guarded by a Hero

family like the plague whenever they weren't actively dealing with the Claude situation, but Rémy glossed right over it as though he'd barely noticed.

"I can't believe my good luck — seeing you twice in one day, Marc!" Annelise exclaimed.

Clothilde almost snickered at how fast her brother's head whipped to look at his betrothed.

"*Really*?" he said, and Annelise smiled as if she hadn't noticed the bite to his tone.

"Oh, yes...we snuck away and had coffee and creamy confections in this intimate little café with cozy booths."

It was almost too funny, seeing her normally unruffled brother get so worked up that a vein in his neck looked like it might just pop, but Clothilde had known that Annelise wouldn't be able to draw out the teasing too long.

"I mean, *Clo and I* had coffee and pastries...across the room from Marc. The chairs at Marc's table didn't look nearly as comfortable, hm-m?"

Marc's voice was amused when he answered, and Clothilde realized that Annelise had put him at ease with her teasing, faster than anything else could have.

"No, ma'am, my chair was a bit spindly...not really made for a big guy. The two of you really looked like you were enjoying your, er, creamy confections, though."

Clothilde backed up so that her bare skin pressed against the front of Marc's tuxedo, and he stiffened behind her.

"Careful, Duchess." His voice was a low growl in her ear, and her nipples went hard.

"*Bon, assez.* I think I've heard enough." Rémy's tone was brisk, but his eyes practically devoured Annelise.

69

"We've come here to work, Clochette. Who would you like for us to charm?"

She took pity on him and sent them off with assignments of a few people to meet and heard Rémy say something to his fiancée about needing to stop by the coatroom as they walked off, which made Annelise's cheeks flame again for some reason.

Marc surprised her by offering her his arm, and she slid her hand along it more than was strictly necessary, appreciating the solid ridges of muscle there. He stood tall and proud next to her, and with the blue dappled light from the huge aquatic tanks that surrounded them playing off the strong lines of his face, he looked like some sort of ocean king.

She was about to tell him so when she spotted a familiar face in the corner of the room. "Is that Brian Clark?" She couldn't stop the immediate surge of affection for the younger man, followed immediately by suspicion. "Should I assume that Tim Barnes is around here somewhere, too?"

Marc stiffened next to her. "Correct on both counts." He sounded uncomfortable. *Good.*

"Not that I'm not happy to see them…" She paused, giving a finger-wave to Brian, who inclined his head with a twitch of his lips before looking stoic again. "But is there any specific reason they're back tonight?"

"Would you believe me if I said they love sea turtles?"

Marc's tone was so dry that Clothilde scoffed, which turned into a delicate snort as she tried to stifle it. "Well, I *would* believe that… Did you know that Tim was a champion sailor before joining the Marines? And Brian takes his little nieces to zoos and aquariums whenever he has leave from his security job?" She turned to look at Marc full-on. "But I don't believe that's why they are here tonight. Is there something you forgot to mention?"

Marc had the good grace to look abashed and unwillingly impressed. "How the hell do you get people to tell you everything? Then remember each detail?"

She didn't want it to, but Marc's compliment warmed her. "*Practice*," she answered simply. "Years and years of endless parties, balls, soirées, luncheons… It's much easier when you genuinely like the people, though."

Marc stepped closer, so she could feel the heat of his body all along her side. "The way you like Clark and Barnes?"

Was that jealousy she heard in his voice? "Don't try to distract me," she huffed.

Marc ran the tip of one rough finger along her spine, leaving fire in its wake, and goosebumps rose on her skin. "If you can scold me about it, I must need to try harder."

She stepped away from him determinedly. "*Non*, just tell me…please."

"I requested that they come back to your personal security detail." His words were low, and honesty rang through them.

"You're genuinely worried." As she spoke, she realized it was true.

"I told you I was," he grumbled. He watched her closely, but she knew that in spite of his attention, he was constantly aware and scanning the room for threats, inconsistencies, any possible disturbance. He was a tiger in a room mostly full of pampered housecats.

She laid her hand on his hard, muscular arm, feeling the power of his strength, undiminished by the different wrapping of his tuxedo. "I heard you...and I trust you to keep me safe."

A muscle worked in his jaw, and he nodded stiffly. "Always," he confirmed, and it made her eyes burn and her chest tighten. She shook her head, desperate to regain her usual equilibrium.

"Well, I can't leave all the mingling to Annelise and Rémy, can I? These guests came to meet a Gaspard, and I won't disappoint them." Her words were deliberately airy but determined.

"No, ma'am," Marc answered, his voice a low growl in her ear, and offered her his arm again.

The party was an unqualified success, and all the guests seemed to be having an excellent time. The setting allowed opportunities not only for amazing food, drinks and dancing, but semi-private alcoves for conversation, and of course, the unique appeal of seeing all the sea creatures after-hours.

Clothilde, still on Marc's arm, was just finishing the rounds of the various alcoves, wanting to be certain she'd spoken to everyone—or at least had given everyone the opening to speak if they wished—when she exclaimed with real happiness at the sight of one of her close friends from boarding school.

"Élodie!" She hurried forward to greet the other woman warmly. "I didn't know you would be here tonight. *Quel plaisir!*"

She hadn't seen her friend nearly as often as she would have liked over the past few years, but they kept in touch via email and the occasional phone call, always trying to fix a time and place to meet up. Élodie Carillon was nearly Clothilde's physical opposite, with silvery-blond hair and bright green eyes, inherited from her Nordic mother, small and curvy where Clothilde was tall and willowy. Clothilde had to bend down a little to hug and kiss her friend, and she inhaled the familiar scent of Élodie's signature perfume.

"You look *exquise, mon amie!*" Clothilde exclaimed, meaning it. For an instant, Clothilde saw something flicker behind Élodie's green eyes, but then the expression vanished and she thought she must have imagined it.

"You too, Clo. That dress is sublime! Not that I'd expect anything less of you. Sorry to show up out of the blue. I only realized last-minute that I'd be able to get away! *Maman* has been so ill, you know…"

Clothilde squeezed her friend's hand in sympathy. Élodie's mother had been unwell for the past two years.

"But she had a couple of good days, so *Papa* convinced me that I should come visit him for a day or two…and, *ben*, here we are!" Élodie opened her arms in a sort of shrug, making the jewels on her wrists and fingers sparkle, and Clothilde noticed for the first time that Élodie's father, Armand Carillon, was standing behind her, along with another man Clothilde didn't recognize. They had been hidden from her sight by the large, concrete support beam as she approached.

"*Monsieur Carillon!* So lovely to see you!" she enthused, although in truth she had never much cared for Élodie's father. He was polite, handsome and unfailingly genteel — and she knew he had been a friend of her own father's when he had been still alive — but something about his over-the-top affection for Élodie and her mother had always rung somehow false to Clothilde. Of course, she had never and would never tell Élodie that.

"Armand, *chérie*. No need to stand on ceremony with someone who has known you since you were but a babe at your mother's breast."

His embrace was warm and firm, and she couldn't wait for it to end.

"Armand," she corrected herself with a smile as she stepped back. "So delighted both you and Élodie could make it. And your...friend?" She turned a dazzling smile to the stranger, who stepped forward into the light as Élodie wrapped proprietary hands around his arm. He moved with fluid grace, but the movements somehow seemed predatory rather than smooth. She mentally kicked herself for seeing danger in every corner, and darted an irritated glance at Marc, who had come to stand close behind her again.

"May I present Raoul de Sancy? Our friend, and my fiancé!" Élodie's face was flushed with pleasure, and Raoul's expression was indulgent. He was handsome, strikingly so, almost like a matinée idol from the American movies of the thirties and forties.

"*Bon Dieu, félicitations*! A thousand congratulations on the happy news!" Clothilde rushed forward again to hug and kiss both Élodie and her fiancé.

"We just got engaged this morning!" Élodie gushed, and the eyes that she turned to the younger man were adoring. "We haven't been together long, but when you know, you just know, right? We can't stand the idea of a long engagement. I mean, who would want to be apart?" She broke off awkwardly, her cheeks flushing red.

Clothilde and Claude had had a very long engagement, and the two girls had once talked about how sensible a plan it was to wait, how it wasn't as if love would change if you waited longer to get married. Clothilde couldn't stand to see her friend embarrassed.

"Just so," she agreed. "When you know, you know. I am so happy for both of you." And she truly was. "Wait! Raoul de Sancy? Are you...Georges de Sancy's son?"

The younger man smiled. "Indeed. I wasn't certain most would remember him."

Clothilde stepped closer, studying him. "Of course! You look just like him...I've seen so many pictures." Georges de Sancy had been her father's best friend in childhood, and they'd remained close until Georges had been killed in a car accident when Clothilde had been very young. She still remembered how her parents had wept.

"You have the advantage over me, then, Mademoiselle Gaspard. My great aunt Jeanne, who raised me in the French countryside, kept no pictures of her sinful nephew." His words were smooth and mocking, but something in his tone was suspiciously tight.

"You'd be more than welcome to visit our family home in Montreal any time I'm there to see the ones we have on display...or I would be happy to go through and choose some to scan or copy. Your father was very dear to mine...to both of my parents. I never met her, but I believe we have some photographs of your mother as well." Her offer was impulsive, but she was utterly sincere, and she could tell that she'd surprised her friend's fiancé. Marc cleared his throat behind her, and Élodie tapped Raoul lightly on his shoulder.

"Enough of this gloomy talk! Clo, aren't you going to introduce us to your companion, as well?" Élodie pouted, but she did it beautifully, and Clothilde had to stifle a laugh. She knew for a fact that Élodie had used to practice that expression in the bathroom mirrors at school.

"Certainly!" Clothilde tugged on Marc's arm, and he stepped forward reluctantly. He'd managed to stay in the background of all the other conversations that evening, and she could tell he would have preferred to stay there now as well. "This is my, um, close friend, Marc Constantin."

The men extended their hands, but Marc tensed visibly when Élodie leaned—much closer than was strictly necessary—and kissed both of his cheeks.

"Always lovely to meet a friend of Clothilde's," Élodie practically purred, but her fiancé looked unperturbed. No matter how short their courtship had been, Clothilde thought, he would have to be used Élodie's outrageous flirtations.

"Nice to meet you, *mademoiselle*," Marc grunted, and Clothilde took pity on him.

"Are you enjoying the party?" she asked the other three.

"Very much so, my dear," Armand answered. "Such a surprisingly exotic location. I would normally never come here, when the masses descend…" He gave a faint shudder of distaste. "But you've really outdone yourself with this private *fête*. Even the animals seem to be enjoying themselves." As if to punctuate his praise, an enormous reddish octopus moved from one side to the other of the tank in front of them, its tentacles mesmerizing.

"Oh, wow! I've never seen one so close," Clothilde exclaimed excitedly, and Raoul and Armand stepped back to let the two women stand closest to the tank.

"Did you know," Raoul started, his voice casual, "that the Giant Pacific Octopus can change color to camouflage itself? And, in spite of weighing up to a hundred pounds or more, it can squeeze into impossibly small spaces. They're really quite astonishing predators, capable of opening jars and valves. They can hide in wait, perfectly disguised, until they pounce on and devour prey as large as sharks."

He moved closer to the two women as he spoke, and Clothilde's neck prickled. *Could he possibly be warning me? Warning us?*

Élodie's laugh was tinkling. "Raoul is such a science nerd. It's a good thing he's so handsome."

Clothilde caught the expression of…not annoyance, but something close to it, in his reflection on the polished glass of the tank before Marc touched her shoulder gently.

"I believe Charles is summoning you for a toast," he murmured, and she turned to him gratefully, suddenly ready to be away from this particular alcove.

"Duty calls," she shrugged helplessly, her smile apologetic.

"But of course," Armand said with a nod.

"I hope we'll see each other very soon. Élodie, let me know if you'll still be in town tomorrow and we can meet up again!"

Élodie smiled. "Absolutely!" Something about her tone seemed forced, but Clothilde told herself she was just being oversensitive again. *Being attacked and nearly murdered by your ex-fiancé has that effect on a girl*, she thought dryly.

# Chapter Six

*Something is going to happen*, Marc thought darkly. Damned if he could put his finger on it, but even as he stood with every appearance of calm, off to one side from the small stage that had been set up, his internal alarms were zinging with tension. There was no reason for it. The evening had been generally calm, the perimeter was secure and no one had so much as been mildly rude. In fact, if he had to guess, Marc thought it would be a blockbuster night for donations. Even now, Clothilde was giving an outstanding speech, funny and poignant, while graciously thanking everyone involved with the charity. But still, his gut told him something was coming...and he'd learned never to ignore his gut instincts for danger. It had saved his ass more times than he could count.

He gave a subtle signal to Clark, who stood across the stage. Clark's nearly imperceptible nod indicated that the younger man would pass along the private message to Barnes. *High alert*, the signal meant. If — no, *when* — shit went down, the two younger soldiers would be ready. It wasn't that Marc didn't trust the other security guys there tonight, but Clark and Barnes had earned his confidence a hundred times over when they'd saved Clothilde and Marina in Vermont. Everyone else could focus on getting information, protecting Clothilde's brother and sister-in-law, even Charles Pinkston, but if it came down to Clothilde and the Chimère, Marc felt strongly that the two younger men would unwaveringly choose Clothilde.

Watching her, Marc felt a flare of pride so deep it went down his bones. She was fucking glorious — all elegant lines in her shimmering gown and so beautiful that it practically burned his eyes to look at her — but she was also fearless. Her determination to help others, to use her influence and give of herself to women and children who were vulnerable, was awe-inspiring. He hated himself all over again for the pain he'd caused her.

He stiffened for a second as another woman crept up the steps on the other side, but then he recognized the main party planner, someone who had worked with Annelise. The normally mousy brunette was surprisingly glamorous in her evening gown...*Rose*, that was her name. She held a thick envelope and waited for Clothilde's nod before darting out to bring whatever urgent message she carried.

Like the pro that she was, Clothilde laughingly worked the surprise into her speech, although Marc still only listened with half an ear, intent on scanning the crowd for any anomaly, any change...anything, really.

"...anonymous donor has, with incredible generosity, agreed to match all donations made at tonight's party, so now is the time to dig deep at his or her expense!" Clothilde's cheeks were flushed with pleasure as she spoke, and she flashed a grateful look at her brother, but instead of the acknowledgment that Marc would have expected, Rémy shrugged his shoulders and looked pensive. *Interesting. The donor isn't her brother.*

"With that in mind, the bidding for the silent auction is ending shortly, and we'll announce the winners right after dessert. *Bon appétit encore, mes dames et messieurs*!" The smile that Clothilde flashed at the crowd was stunning, and if Marc hadn't spent so long studying her every expression, he would have thought she was thrilled, but the levity didn't quite reach her eyes. Still, the crowd applauded and drifted off happily to the dessert stations and high-top tables arranged throughout the space.

As Clothilde approached his side of the stage, her expression was thoughtful. As she slipped her arm into his, almost without thinking, some primal part of him cheered, even as the feel of her against him made other parts of his body stand to attention as well.

"Is that an unusual donation?" he murmured, close to her ear.

Clothilde looked up at him, but he could tell she was still puzzling it out. "Not the practice, *non*. It's pretty common to have a donation match, but to be a surprise and for the whole evening…it's bound to be quite a large amount, and I have no real idea who it was, if it wasn't one of my brothers."

She raised the crystal tumbler in her other hand to her mouth, taking a long sip of sparkling water, and alarm bells sang out in Marc's mind. He grabbed her wrist and pulled the drink away from her lips.

"Where did you get that?" He knew his question was harsh, but he didn't care. Earlier, he'd watched the bartender open new bottles to prepare her last two drinks, never taking his eyes off the servers to ensure that no subtle movement escaped him.

Clothilde's brown eyes grew large and alarmed, and the bones of her wrist felt small in his hand. He forced himself to ease up on his grip.

"There were unopened bottles at the podium. I was thirsty, so I just poured one for myself." Her words were halting, and he hated that he'd made her afraid. *Again.* Shitty bodyguard he was turning out to be.

It was probably fine. He knew he was being overbearing, overly cautious, basically overly everything at this point. The sparkling water was the fancy kind that Clothilde preferred, which came in sealed glass bottles — very difficult to tamper with. But still...not impossible. And putting something in the glass would be ballsy, since Clothilde wasn't the only person who had used the podium. He was probably reading more into this than he should, but he was fucking close to the edge with her so exposed.

He forced his heart to slow its frantic beating, and he plucked the glass from her hand, setting it down on a nearby table.

"It's okay," he said with a calm that he didn't feel and forced a small smile. "Just let me get all your drinks from now on, all right?"

Clothilde inclined her head. "Of course. I just...I always get so warm when I give speeches."

Marc was surprised. "You looked pretty damn calm and collected from where I was standing."

Her answering smile was wry. "Having stage fright is terribly inconvenient for a Gaspard, *tu peux imaginer,* so I trained myself a long time ago to ignore it. Well, at least to look like I don't have it anymore. But my body isn't so easily fooled, and I always have to drink something right after."

As she spoke, he could see her pulse fluttering quickly in her neck, and he kicked himself for never noticing the subtle signs of her anxiety. Her serene expression never wavered, but tiny droplets of sweat beaded on her upper lip and at her hairline, and there was a nearly imperceptible tremble in her movements. Touching her as he was, though, he could feel it. Why would he think that a former model and society 'it' girl would have this reaction, though? He wondered if he'd been misreading even more about Clothilde than he'd thought.

He studied her again, and her cheeks looked flushed, too.

"Want me to snag you a fresh bottle and we can head outside to get some air?" he suggested.

"I *am* a little warm," she acknowledged, her expression guarded but grateful. "*Oui*, that would be great."

It shouldn't have, but her trust, especially after the strain of their earlier conversation, made his heart soar. He guided her to the outdoor walkway, grabbing a sealed bottle of sparkling water at one of the beverage stations on the way. At first, the bartender had looked like he wanted to protest, but something in Marc's expression must have warned him, because he backed right the hell off. *Good*, Marc thought savagely.

As soon as they got out of the heavy aquarium doors to the harbor walk area, the stiff breeze that had turned slightly colder buffeted them, tearing at Clothilde's artfully mussed coiffure, making it look more windblown. Her eyes as she turned back to him didn't look upset, though, but instead gleamed with her pleasure. She gave a delicate shiver.

"Cold, baby?" he rumbled, unable to stop himself from speaking intimately while they were alone.

"No...feels fresh. Really good after that stuffy room."

Marc hadn't thought that the aquarium was particularly stuffy, but the pleasure in Clothilde's tone was unmistakable. A slight noise made him look back where, he noted with satisfaction, Barnes had silently followed them out. He inclined his head in approval toward the younger soldier before he twisted the cap off the water, holding it out to her.

"Is it okay without a glass?" he asked.

Clothilde raised her eyebrow. "*You're* worried about keeping up appearances? You surprise me, *mon grand*." Her tone was teasing, and she held the cold bottle up to her forehead in an unconscious gesture. He'd seldom seen her be so casual with anyone but her family, and it warmed him. Gave him hope that maybe she could come to forgive him. Not that he deserved it...deserved her, but he wished...

"No," he countered. "I'm worried about *you*." He cleared his throat of the tightness that had suddenly formed there. "You want something, *I'll* give it to you...do it for you."

She stepped closer to him, so that he could feel the heat of her body next to his. The tips of her spectacular breasts, hardened in the night air, were scant inches from touching him. He ached to close that small gap, to feel her against him just once more. The yearning was so strong that he clenched his fists at his side and drew in a deep breath. Big mistake, since he only drew in more of her unique, ethereal scent...like a dream of everything that was good, everything that he couldn't have.

"Marc," she breathed, and her expression was soft, mirroring his own tender feelings. When she looked at him like that, he couldn't remember why he was supposed to keep his distance. He wouldn't have remembered his own name if she hadn't just spoken it.

They reached for each other at the same time, and he inadvertently bumped her, *hard*, making her wobble on her high heels so that she fell against him, forcing him to catch her in an awkward hug and take a step back, more out of surprise than because of the force of her slight weight. *Real smooth, Constantin*, he berated himself. The pleasure of the feel of her curves flush against him quickly banished all rational thought, making every cell zing and his heart thump out a loud rhythm. *Rat-a-tat-tat-tat*.

It took him a split second longer than it should have. *Shit, it's not my heart*, flashed into his brain. Bullets were hitting the thick metal railing where Clothilde's body had leaned only an instant earlier.

*Vachement cool, Clochette*, Clothilde scolded herself for tumbling into Marc with all the grace of a drunken camel. She'd nearly knocked him over, dropping her water bottle, then the world went haywire. Everything happened so fast that it took her mind a few seconds to catch up with her body. There was a loud sort of rapping, Marc's entire body went hard like solid steel, then he practically threw her up into the air and caught her in a hybrid fireman's carry. She couldn't spare much of a thought as to how freakishly strong it made him that the movement had seemed utterly effortless, because all her energy was suddenly taken up with trying to catch her breath as he set off at a fast jog, jarring her entire body with every step, lungs and stomach included, and she needed every neuron to try to remember how to breathe. *Que diable? What the hell?*

Marc touched his ear with his free arm — *how the heck does he have a free arm while he's carrying me?* — and his words were harsh, vibrating with anger. No, not anger...*rage*.

"Shots fired. I repeat, shots have been fired from above. Exact location of shooter is unknown."

*What? Shots fired?* A cold chill crept over Clothilde's skin in spite of the warmth of Marc's shoulder and arm, seeping deeper into her body until it felt as if it touched her soul itself. Someone was shooting at her...had nearly *hit* her. Vaguely, she realized Marc was still talking.

"...securing the building...transit to secondary position." His voice was still harsh, businesslike, but it wasn't cold. It whipped with his barely leashed fury. He might be acting calm, but Marc was deeply affected.

Clothilde shook off the frozen feeling, forcing her body and mind to focus. In spite of how fast they were running, Marc was barely breathing heavily, his footsteps steady and unfaltering. It was a beautiful evening, and they were in a popular area, so close to the harbor, but luckily nobody passed them too closely on the path. She recognized the footpath as one that led over to the next pier. She wiggled in a silent request to be let down.

Marc shifted her in his arms so she could see him more clearly and tightened his grip around her. "No, baby," he said, and she wondered if he knew how tender he sounded. She thought that she wouldn't tell him if she wanted him to keep talking like that. "It's faster if I carry you...your hip."

She knew he was right. She might be healed, but her hip and leg would never be the same...never be normal. And she still wore ridiculous high heels. So why did his words make her flush with shame?

"I'll take any excuse to hold you, Duchess," he added, trying for a tight smile that she could only see enough of out of the corner of her eye to know that he failed miserably. She loved that he tried, anyway.

"Where's the secondary position?" she asked.

"Close," he answered, his tone clipped, and she saw they were headed to one of the private slip areas.

It cost a fortune to have a slip there, right in the heart of the city, and the ships that rose around them were stunning. In fact, one of them looked almost exactly like... "The *Sans Souci*," she murmured. Luc's luxurious sailboat...really, like a small sail yacht. She'd thought it was still in Nice or Cannes. The passerelle was already down and another very young man with a distinctly military bearing guarded it with watchful eyes. He stood up straighter as Marc and Clothilde approached.

Marc's pace didn't slow one iota as he jogged right along the gangway and up onto the ship, not pausing as they passed the younger man, who followed them at a brisk pace until they were into the bridge and he stood at the doorway to the companionway, half-in and half-out in a pose that was clearly still watchful.

Marc didn't speak but quirked one of his expressive eyebrows.

"Everything is ready, sir. And I got confirmation that Rémy Gaspard has been notified of his sister's safety and status. You can cast off as soon as the others arrive."

Marc nodded tersely. "Should only be a minute." He gestured at his ear, implying he was talking to them. "Appreciate it."

The young man who'd been waiting on the boat flushed with pleasure at the compliment, although his expression remained impassive. "It was an honor, uh, sir." He'd obviously started to say something else but trailed off.

Clothilde realized that this had happened before. Several of the young military types who were supposedly part of Marc's private security crew had started to call him something else…then stopped themselves. She'd always thought it was because Marc was some sort of military hero—in fact, she'd read somewhere that he'd had to retire because his involvement in a huge mission had become public, his name and face being splashed on newsfeeds around the world—but something about this seemed different. Again, a strange image of a dark hospital hallway flashed into her mind's eye.

"You'd better stay aboard, soldier," Marc answered. "Don't think the shooter's going after other targets, but whoever he is, he's good…*really* good. A professional wouldn't hesitate to intercept you." His tone was grim for all that it was businesslike.

The younger man inclined his head in acknowledgment. He was young, but the total lack of fear and steel grit she could read in his expression told Clothilde that he was more experienced than she'd thought.

"Are we going somewhere?" she asked, raising one eyebrow in inquiry. Marc tightened his arms around her as if he were reluctant to let her go, but then gently set her down so that she was steady on her high heels on the dark wooden flooring of the yacht's cockpit.

First Barnes then Clark slipped into the room, surprisingly stealthy and unruffled, given that they must have basically run from the aquarium as well. Marc gave a grunt of satisfaction.

"Now we are. A jaunt to a little remote island off the coast of Northern Maine. Let's get you settled in, sweetheart. Barnes, we good here with a crew of three?"

Barnes had already stood tall, but now he straightened even farther, and she had the impression of him coming to full attention. "Yes, sir," he confirmed.

"Luc Gaspard confirmed that all the glass is bulletproof, and the hull around the cabins is reinforced as well." Marc's words were a surprise to her, but really, thinking about it, and all the dangers that her family had faced in the past, it wasn't so odd. Clothilde did wonder when Luc, who gave the impression of being carefree, had become so safety-conscious.

"Understood, sir," Barnes answered.

"Good," Marc replied, and slid his fingers from where he'd left them on Clothilde's bare shoulder down her arm to hold her hand. There was nothing inappropriate about it, but it was a curiously intimate gesture. "I'm taking Clothilde to the main cabin, then. Come get me if there's an emergency, and *only* if there's an emergency. Otherwise, I'll be back up in a while."

They shouldn't have, but his words—and the raw command behind them—made Clothilde give a little shiver, goosebumps rising on her exposed skin. *Maybe*

*I'm colder than I realized?* she wondered. Even as she had the thought, she swayed against Marc, and he circled his arm around her, pulling her tightly against his side to stabilize her.

"What is it, Clo?"

She ached to hear the worry in his voice.

"Nothing...just lightheaded all of a sudden." She waved her hand as if to wave off his concerns, but instead of being reassuring, the movement was wobbly

"Shock," Marc answered tersely. Without warning, he swung her into his arms again, this time in a bridal carry, and headed down the steps to the cabins with her. She only had an instant to be thankful that it was such a luxury ship that it had wide hallways and stairways before he'd carried her into the expansive master suite. The fabrics and decorations were decadent — Luc never did anything by halves — and she had only the impression of an enormous bed before Marc was laying her onto it with as much care as if she'd been a fragile, blown-glass vase like the ones her youngest brother enjoyed collecting from Venice.

He rubbed the back of his neck in the gesture she recognized as one that he always made when he was uncomfortable, subtly shifting his weight from one foot to the other. "You should get under the covers, baby, and I'll get you some orange juice. Then I can leave you alone for a little while...although I can't go far."

The vibration of the engines was a low purr as they started up, but there must have been some sort of surge since the ship jerked, forcing Marc to lose his balance. He almost caught himself in an acrobatic dance worthy of a circus performer, but he snagged his toe on the rug and he fell heavily on top of her with an embarrassed grunt.

"Shit," he breathed, and the word was so close to her ear that it made her hair flutter. "I'm so sorry."

He'd knocked the wind out of her when his weight had landed on top of her, so at first she could just croak, but when she could suck in a lungful of air, she exhaled on a giggle. He had looked so incredibly ridiculous with his arms pinwheeling and his face a mask of intense concentration.

"Oh, God, are you choking, sweetheart?" Marc half-rolled off her, and his eyes blazed with deep worry.

She shook her head and tried to reply, but between having had the air pressed from her and the uncontrollable mirth, it came out as a gasp. "No..." she wheezed. "Fine."

His expression was dubious.

She forced herself to try to take deep breaths. In some part of her brain, she knew that her body was just releasing some tension through amusement...but she wasn't sure she succeeded very well. She turned more toward Marc, burying her face in his chest, all hard muscles, and breathing in his comforting, warm scent. The material of his tux was sightly scratchy, so unlike the custom suits the men of her family and Claude had always worn.

"Are you... Baby, did I make you *cry*?" Marc sounded anguished, and the real pain in his tone sobered her like nothing else could have.

She shook her head against him and felt his arms go around her. He trailed a hand in long strokes up and down her bare back, and she didn't think he was even aware of the movement.

"I'm fine," she answered.

She could feel Marc shaking his head. "No...goddamn it, you're not fine. Someone got in shots at you — really fucking close shots — on my watch. You shouldn't have to live this way, baby. We're supposed to be able to protect you... *I'm* supposed to be able to protect you." Clothilde could hear his heart beat, much faster than usual. She hadn't been the only one affected by the attack.

When she tried, he let her pull away an inch or so, but no farther.

"You *did* protect me, Marc. I don't know how you could run so fast carrying me, as if I weighed nothing at all."

He scoffed, but he didn't sound displeased. "You don't weigh much, Clo, and you felt amazing in my arms again...no matter why you were there." He cleared his throat uncomfortably, as if realizing what he'd revealed. "Are you hurt? Were you crying because I landed on something painful?"

Clothilde flushed warmly. Even now, her amusement threatened to flare again, and it was in such contrast with Marc's serious tone that she was embarrassed.

"I wasn't crying," she admitted in a low voice.

Marc sighed heavily. "Baby, I felt you tense, then you were shaking against me. You don't have to lie to spare my feelings." He started to pull away, but she put one hand onto his side and he halted mid-movement.

"It's totally inappropriate but...I was laughing."

Marc was still and silent for a long moment, so she rushed to continue.

"I know I should be terrified — and *putain*, that attack was frightening — but when you danced around like a drunken bear on a tightrope, trying not to fall on top of me, then did it anyway, *ben*..." Even as she trailed off, she couldn't keep the grin from her face. "I'm sorry I laughed at you. Perhaps I'm a terrible person, but I can't let you feel bad thinking I was crying."

Marc shook his head slowly, and she braced herself. Even after all the time since she'd been with Claude, she could still hear his voice sometimes in her head. *I thought that you, as a Gaspard, would at least know how to act, Clothilde, but you were as graceful as an ox tonight...stupid as a cow...clumsy and fat as a hippo.* It had never mattered to Claude how much weight she lost from her naturally slender frame, or how successful she was, either at modeling or in her charity work. It was never enough...*would* never have been. She knew that now, and that the things he'd said weren't true, but after years with her treacherous ex—believing that, every day, continued to be a challenge.

Instead of a criticism, when he spoke, Marc's words were full of wonder. "I always forget that you have a backbone of pure steel, sweetheart, but I should remember who I'm dealing with. I'm so glad you weren't crying...and it's normal to laugh. I've seen some brothers-in-arms have the same reaction after danger has passed. It lets off tension." His small smile grew wry. "Plus, I bet I looked hilarious."

Clothilde was so stunned at his reaction when she'd braced herself for the worst, that she almost didn't hear his next words.

"Let me get you that orange juice now." It was an eminently reasonable statement, but when he moved to pull away, she reacted instinctively.

"No...stay with me, on the bed."

# Chapter Seven

Marc wondered if he'd been injured after all and was lying on a hospital gurney somewhere having a vivid fantasy about Clothilde, because there was no fucking way she meant what he thought she meant. If, by chance, she had actually intended to tell him to stay in bed with her, for any reason, he was going to have to do the noble thing and leave anyway.

Most of the time, he was okay with being a good guy. He was the guy who warned all the younger recruits when they were drinking too much, when they were pushing too hard and he drove young women home from parties with no expectation of anything in return. His own ex-wife had accused him of being more committed to his sense of honor and duty than he'd ever been to her, and he feared very much that she might have been right. With Clothilde, for the first time — as well as the second, third and twentieth time — he questioned his honor and whether he wanted to put duty above all else. *No, Constantin, just admit it to yourself...you question whether you want to put those things above* her.

The object of his thoughts—his obsession—was flushed and stretched out beside him, the surprisingly soft curves of her lithe body pressed all down his side. The danger they'd been in had banked his ever-present desire for her. No, it was more than desire—his desperate, gnawing need for her. With her words, though, and the vulnerable expression in her eyes, his passion came roaring back like a freight train, smashing through his defenses. *She's vulnerable, asshole*. The thought calmed him, if only a little, and he concentrated on remembering to put her needs first.

"You might need sugar, sweetheart." He tried for a gentle, reasonable tone, but he feared it came out as a growl. He congratulated himself on being able to think of anything but the monster erection that strained for her with a mind of its own.

An adorable little wrinkle appeared between her perfect eyebrows—and every goddamn thing about Clothilde was exquisite. "I don't feel dizzy anymore, but if you think I need to drink it... Come back and hold me again, though?" Her expression was open and somehow pleading, and he didn't think he could have refused her anything at all in that instant. He would have sold his very soul, and he thought that Cob would have understood.

Marc knew that Clothilde didn't like for anyone to see the softness underneath her glittering armor. She trusted few people, and he was only just now realizing how deeply he'd betrayed that trust—even more than he'd known—when he'd abandoned her before. The courage she was displaying in reaching out again amazed him...humbled him. He knew he still wasn't worthy of it, but dammit, he would do everything he possibly could to give her what she needed.

"Yes," he breathed, "I'll hold you. Anything, baby…just ask and it's yours, if it's something within my power to give."

Her dark eyes went soft and liquid, and he felt ten feet tall in the light of her admiration. Her expression flashed with sudden amusement.

"I mean, I was happy with the idea of a juice and your arms around me, maybe feeling your hands on me…but now I'm thinking it could be a good time to secure the promise that you'll donate a kidney or bone marrow, too—you know, just in case."

He knew she was teasing, but he answered seriously. "I would do that for you and more… Duchess, I would gladly shield you from harm with my own body, always. There's nothing that I don't want to give you." He turned away before she could see his expression, afraid of what she might find there, and he crossed the thick carpet in three long, muffled steps to the small bar he'd noted on the way into the room. He cursed himself for saying so much, and he could only blame how raw he was feeling after nearly watching Clothilde be shot to death in front of him. Any one of those shots, had it struck her, could have been fatal.

He and his team been prepared for an attack, but they'd somehow still missed the shooter, and that didn't say anything good. They'd done a widespread sweep of the area in advance, which meant that the attacker was almost certainly a party guest or employee. Since attendees and staff had all been carefully vetted—although they hadn't had time to do a deep dive on some of the lower-risk guests with the limited advance warning—he and his team must have missed something critical. That error had nearly cost Clothilde her life, and he found the idea of a world without her bright flame in it…barren. *Unthinkable.*

He forced himself to focus on something else until he calmed down. They were executing a good plan B, and they should be safe for the moment. He could deal with any fallout later, when Clothilde was totally secure. For now, he was going to concentrate on finding a bottle of orange juice in the minifridge.

*What kind of a guy is Luc Gaspard that he keeps a full bar in his yacht bedroom?* he asked himself. *The kind of guy who owns this kind of ship*, Marc supposed, mentally answering his own question. Clothilde's brother had been more than willing to lend the ship, or anything else, to Marc for the protection of his sister, though. Marc had spent a good amount of time with both Pierre and Rémy, but Luc was still a bit of wild card, since he was mainly based in Europe now, returning to Montreal and Boston periodically but always hurrying back as soon as he could to run all the European branches, which were headquartered in Paris.

By all accounts, Luc was a genius at business and enjoyed it, along with a fabulous lifestyle. And yet…all the Gaspard siblings had been putting on a show for *la presse* since they'd been young, to allow themselves a measure of privacy. In light of that and the fact that Luc seemed to be the closest brother to Clothilde, whom she called frequently and went to meet up with whenever she could, Marc wondered if Luc's private persona was dramatically different.

In fact, based on some interesting gaps in his background, Marc suspected Luc had hidden something, even from his own siblings. Marc had decided not to pursue any additional information on the incident, since it didn't seem related at all to the Chimère, and the woman who'd been involved was dead. However, in light of the increased danger to Clothilde, he worried he might have been too hasty.

Without even realizing what he'd been doing, he noticed he'd poured the orange juice into a crystal glass—*who keeps crystal on a* ship, *for the love of God?*— and he crossed back to the bed where Clothilde appeared to be dozing. Her eyelids fluttered open and the pure tenderness and welcome in them made his heart clench. He might be a bastard and he certainly didn't deserve her, but he would remember that expression until the day he died.

"Marc," she whispered, and his cock strained dangerously against the zipper of his rented tux.

"Got your juice, baby," he murmured. "Want to sit up a little bit?"

She shimmied, her full breasts bouncing in the bodice of her gown as she was obviously hampered by the fabric. Marc stifled a groan and tried not to stare, even though he knew he was failing miserably. As soon as she was semi-upright, he held the glass to her lips. She took a long sip—since he kind of forced her to— and her half-smile when he lowered the glass was bemused.

"I can do things for myself, you know." She raised her eyebrows.

"I know," he said. "I just…really want to do something to take care of you right now." His voice was strained, and he thought again of all the times he'd almost lost her, not just tonight, but also when she'd been kidnapped by Claude de Voltin and poisoned the infamous night of the party. Hell, he would never have met her if she hadn't fought so hard for survival the night of her near-fatal car accident.

"I understand," she said, so softly that he had to strain his ears a bit with the background hum of the motors. "Did you mean what you said, just now?"

"I'm sorry," he answered. "I shouldn't have said that."

"So you didn't mean it," she said, her voice going flat. And just like that, he knew he was going to dig himself in deeper.

He raised his left hand to stroke the warm satin of her cheek. "No, I meant every word." He let his sincerity ring through in his words. "I shouldn't have said it, though, because no matter what I want to give you, there are things I just can't."

Clothilde's expression had brightened, but now it grew wary. "If I ask you a question, will you answer honestly?"

Marc sighed, hating his oaths, promises and even his honor at that moment. "If I can."

"Understood." She nodded slowly. "If you had a choice, would you have left me that morning, after my bad allergic reaction? And stayed away for months?"

Marc considered what he was allowed to say...he was already right on the fucking line between obeying orders and insubordination. He was lucky Menzies — who he still thought was a bastard but maybe not the entirely hopeless dickwad he'd once assumed — hadn't already strung him up by his balls. He decided to be honest, damn the consequences. Clothilde deserved to know the truth, or at least the most he could say.

"If I had a choice, I would never leave you." It was a naked statement, and he felt utterly exposed.

Clothilde sucked in a breath, and her eyes grew shiny. She looked like she wanted to ask more, like if he hadn't wanted to leave, why had he done it. Maybe, as his ex-wife had, she would simply call him a liar. He braced himself when she opened her mouth to speak, but her words surprised him.

"Thank you," she said, the two little words imbued with deep gratitude. "And I know you probably can't tell me more, and I think…I think I'm okay with that." She gave a dry laugh. "Or, not okay, but I think that's enough for now, if that's all I get to have."

He heaved out a breath he didn't realize he'd been holding, and he didn't think he'd ever seen her look more beautiful. He was proven wrong in the next instant as a delicate flush tinged her cheekbones and she licked her lips in an unconsciously seductive gesture that he'd seen her make before, only when she was in private. He waited for her to continue, but she didn't.

"I don't deserve that, sweetheart, but I don't think I care right now," he answered honestly. "Did you want to say something else?"

Clothilde looked uncomfortable, and her breathing grew more rapid, making her bosom practically strain against the straps of her dress. He marveled again at what a contradiction she was. Her public persona was cool, haughty, elegant, confident. She played the part so well, and had such a genuinely dry sense of humor, that he thought she likely even fooled her a family a good amount of the time. Underneath it all, though, she was protecting herself.

With a bolt of clarity, he wondered if she had much real experience at all with men. She'd been engaged to her childhood sweetheart, so she obviously had some knowledge, but given the way she'd described how Claude had treated her, he suspected she might have very limited amount.

"Aren't you, uh...? Do you still want—?"

It was adorable how flustered she was getting, the society darling that some people called the Ice Queen.

"To hold you? God, baby, more than anything...but are you okay with knowing I have to keep some things from you?"

Clothilde gave a shaky nod. "I see you, Marc, in spite of what you can't say. Maybe I shouldn't, but I'm trusting you. I just want to feel better."

# Chapter Eight

As if her words had lit a fire behind him, Marc set down the glass and stretched out next to her with flattering alacrity. Clothilde knew she might be making a mistake, but she was so tired of guarding herself...so tired of feeling alone, missing Marc, wishing he were with her. She realized now that while she'd been punishing him, she'd been punishing herself, too.

Oh, she knew she could have chosen someone else — *bon Dieu*, there had been a lot of offers from other men — but she genuinely liked Marc. In spite of how much his actions and desertion had upset her, she still trusted him, more than anyone else. More than that, though, he was the first man who she felt really saw her...*Clothilde*, not the youngest Gaspard, or her face or body. His every action, every expression, made it obvious that he felt affection for her...maybe tenderness, maybe nothing else, but she wasn't sure that she cared. Right now, she just wanted the comfort and warmth of that affection. She wanted to be wrapped up in it.

"You wanted my arms around you?" he rumbled, as if he'd heard her thoughts.

She breathed in his outdoor-fresh scent from his bowtie and shirtfront and nodded against his chest, sighing with pleasure as he pulled her even closer into his body with his strong arms, hard with muscles.

"You wanted my hands on you...*maybe*." His words, echoing hers from a moment before, were a deep murmur directly into her ear, and goosebumps of pleasure rose all over her skin. When his hands, warm and hard with calluses, stroked gently over her back, she shivered at the sensation.

"Cold?" he asked, his breath fanning the downy hairs on her cheek and neck.

"N-no," she managed to stammer out. "Feels so good...so right," she sighed. Surprisingly, even as his touches, which were relatively innocent, inflamed her passion, she felt the cold knot of tension that had built up in the pit of her stomach earlier that night—in fact, maybe much earlier than that—was starting to melt. She knew it probably wouldn't go away, not as long as she kept her secret shame from him, but she would do that as long as she could.

"I'm glad, sweetheart... Feels right to me, too. Let me make you feel good, take care of you."

He ran his fingers, so different from her smooth skin, all along her bare shoulders and back, but he paused when he reached the straps of her dress.

"Are these straps hurting you? They feel like they're digging right into your flesh."

She thought about lying, because she didn't want to him to stop what he was doing. She must have been silent for too long because he spoke again.

"Tell me the truth," he urged. "I think we have enough misunderstandings between us already, don't we?"

"The straps *are* really pulling tight," she confessed. "But I'm used to things being uncomfortable, especially dresses and shoes."

Marc's grunt was displeased. "Not with me, baby."

His demanding tone warmed her. "I can't take my dress off, though. I'm not, um, wearing anything except my…uh, panties underneath," she confessed. "The bra is, sort of, built into the bodice."

He tensed, and his voice sounded strangled when he answered her. "We can take your dress off and I can just tuck you in and walk away, or I can try to find you a T-shirt or something to wear…"

For some reason, his consideration…and the knowledge that he would just get up and walk away, even as she could feel his growing hardness pressing against her hip, made her feel bold—more daring than she'd ever been with Claude or anyone else—except maybe with Marc himself on that long-ago car ride, but she always seemed to see those memories as if through a haze, which she blamed on the allergic reaction.

"What if we take off my dress and you just keep doing what you were doing?" she suggested, and her voice was low and sultry…more sensuous than she'd known it could sound.

"God, yes…if you're sure?" He paused with his fingers practically hooked under the straps of her dress.

"I'm sure," she confirmed, practically pressing her shoulder blades into his hands.

"I know I shouldn't do this."

Her heart sank at his words but bobbed up again when he continued.

"But damn if I'm going to refuse you anything. I promise I'll keep everything on, sweetheart. This is for you."

She made a throaty sound that came from somewhere deep inside her chest, and he started to push the straps down, but with how tightly they had been pulled by her movements on the bed, they both snapped off with muffled *thwaps*. The relief of the pressure off her shoulders and against her breasts was wonderful, but Marc looked apologetic as he half-reclined back onto his side.

"Sorry, baby… I think I ruined your dress." The disconnected, bejeweled strap still hung from one of his fingers. It had been a lovely gown, handmade by one of the most famous Parisian design houses, and she couldn't have cared less in that moment.

"I have others," she answered softly, smiling at how funny he looked, his bowtie askew and holding part of her dress.

"I'll just bet you do." He grinned. "But I find myself growing inordinately fond of this particular one."

Her heart gave an extra thump at the earnest admiration she read in his eyes.

"We can fix it, then, but you better be careful with the rest," she whispered, holding his gaze.

"I plan to be careful with you, Clo," he answered, and she knew he wasn't only talking about her gown. "Turn a little so I can get the zipper," he ordered, and she felt the same goosebumps rise on her arms at the command in his voice. Weird, because she had never liked it when Claude had commanded her to do things.

Well, maybe at first, when they'd still been in high school, it had felt exciting, and wonderful to finally be the sole object of the attentions of such a handsome, popular boy who she'd always had a crush on from the time she'd figured out what crushes were. But later, it had been a lead-up to his cruelty. With Marc, though, she loved how he took charge, demanding but still considerate.

She pushed all thoughts of anything else from her head when she turned away as Marc asked, and he slid down the zipper of the dress with aching tenderness, tugging the fabric of her bodice down gently, before sliding the whole thing down and off her legs, leaving her bare but for a very small scrap of blue lace that was sort of a hybrid between a thong and bikini briefs.

She heard the swish of the fabric falling to the carpet, then Marc sucked in a sharp breath.

"*Beautiful*," he breathed, his tone reverent.

She turned her head to look at his expression, over her shoulder. She wasn't sure what she expected, but the naked appreciation surprised her. Marc looked at her like she was a princess...holding his favorite dessert. He devoured her with his eyes, and of all the admiration she'd ever received, on the runway, from photographers, admirers, would-be boyfriends...nothing even came close to how gorgeous and sensual Marc's expression made her feel.

She turned back toward him but felt suddenly shy and started to raise her arms to cover her breasts as they bobbled slightly with her movement, but Marc's touch on her forearm stopped her.

"Don't cover up, sweetheart. You're...perfection." His eyes glowed blue in the dim light, filled with passion but also tenderness. She thought she could get addicted to seeing that expression on his face. He focused his stare on her breasts and gave a harsh growl.

"Shit, baby, your dress left red marks. I should have made sure you were comfortable as soon as we got in here."

He looked fierce and protective, reaching to touch what she noticed were fiery red indentations from the underwire into her white flesh. As soon as his hands connected with her skin, though, she couldn't help a gasp. Her nipples tightened to hard points.

"The marks…will go away," she answered, trying to sound reassuring but instead sort of panting.

Seemingly oblivious, he brushed his fingers over the marks gently, frowning. "It sounds like this has happened before."

When one of his wrists grazed the very tips of one breast, she moaned, and his gaze shot to her face.

"Did I hurt you?"

She shook her head mutely, not trusting herself to speak for a moment. "No…they're just…*so sensitive.*"

As if she'd flipped a switch, his expression went from concern to desire, and his eyes went heavy-lidded.

"Really…so if I do this?" He moved his hands so they cupped each breast, and flicked his thumbs over the tips of her nipples with feather-light touches. She practically quivered out of his arms.

"Aah…so good," she breathed.

"God, you're gorgeous," he answered, and it was all the warning she had before he covered her mouth with his. It was no tentative kiss, but a conquering of her mouth with his, a plundering—and she reveled in it. She tasted champagne and the unique spicy taste that was Marc, and she opened her mouth to allow him in, stroking his tongue against hers, making her core go liquid with desire. He alternated deep strokes with shallower ones, brushing the tip of his tongue and lips over hers, until she was writhing and bucking underneath him. With his hands already cupping her breasts, he began a rhythmic stroking in time with his kisses, and she let her legs fall open so he could more easily lie on top of her, his hardness pressed against the needy heat at the V of her thighs. He thrust against her, his length rubbing her wonderfully, even through the layers of his clothes and her thin underwear, and before she realized what she was doing, she was gasping, clutching him with her arms and her legs.

"You're so sensual, sweetheart...so responsive." Marc's voice was a harsh whisper, and he squeezed her breasts with the just right amount of light pressure, not too hard, before circling her nipples again with his fingers. She bucked wildly underneath him, crying out as her bundle of nerves rubbed against his length. The sensation of him, fully clothed, against her naked flesh was surprisingly erotic.

"Yes," she agreed, not really conscious of what she was saying. "So sensitive for you... I dreamed of the way you touched me, that night in the car...the way you sucked me."

Marc's eyes went white-hot, and she flushed at what she'd revealed.

"You thought about that? Dreamed about it?"

She almost looked away but he continued, and the intensity in his voice made her look at him again.

"Me too, Clo... I thought about it so much. I jerked off every night for months, thinking...no, *remembering* you...how it was between us...the way you came apart in my arms."

Clothilde felt the heat rise into her cheeks and chest, and all the way throughout his body at his raw words and the image they conjured. She should possibly be offended, but she...really wasn't. The idea of him touching himself, remembering her, was unbelievably hot. *And weren't you doing the same thing?* The little voice of honesty inside her head was unflinchingly honest.

"I thought about you," she acknowledged, and he rewarded her with more kisses and strokes of his fingers. He pressed kisses to her cheeks, then began to nibble down her jaw and neck, so she turned her head with a gasp. "Even when I made myself stop thinking about you, I dreamed about you," she confessed, and he moved his left hand down to circle caresses around her hip. She hadn't been able to escape his memory at night, when he visited her dreams, making her awaken drenched in sweat and gasping for relief. "I wished you were with me," she whispered, and she wasn't sure if he heard until he raised his blond head, holding her gaze with a fierce intensity that nearly scared her.

"I wanted to be there, and I'm here now," he answered, and it sounded like a vow. He sealed it with a searing kiss on her lips, then lowered his head to her breast at the same time as he reached his hand into her panties and found her dripping folds with one achingly gentle finger.

The simultaneous sensations were overwhelming, sending her careening over the edge of bliss. She trembled and held him to her, and he tenderly sucked and stroked her until the last of her quivering subsided. She was a little embarrassed by how quickly he'd made her come, but when he looked up at her again, she saw nothing but admiration in his expression.

"You're so fucking gorgeous when you come, baby…like a goddamn sunrise."

She giggled. "A sunrise?" she asked.

He quirked his mouth up on one side in a lop-sided half-smile. "I never said I was a poet. That's just what you remind me of — sunrise on the beach, when it's just starting to get lighter, then all of a sudden you're surrounded by pink and orange and red and purple and you think you can see God himself…" He trailed off, clearly embarrassed.

Her heart clenched in her chest, and she leaned to kiss him. "That sounded pretty poetic to me," she teased. She reached her hand down to find his hardness, but he guided her away.

"No, sweetheart, tonight is only about making you feel good…not me."

Her relief was intense. She could keep her secret for a little bit longer, then. For an instant, she thought he looked…guilty? *Why would Marc feel guilty about what we're doing?* But then the expression passed like it had never been there, and he just looked sweet and sexy.

"Do you feel good now, or do you maybe want a little more touching?" He moved his hand, still trapped in her panties, so that he dipped his middle finger into her passage, so wet now that the tip slid right in. She quivered and trembled at the sensation, torn between trepidation and arousal.

"Interesting," he teased. "I think your pretty little pussy would like some more attention, but I'd better take a look to be sure, hm?"

She laughed nervously, tensing his finger inadvertently so that he withdrew the tip, making her moan. Marc suited his words to actions and slid down the bed, bending his head to her core and sliding her underwear to the side.

She squirmed uncomfortably at his close scrutiny and tried to close her legs.

"Stop teasing... I know men don't really like doing that. It's just made up for movies."

Marc lifted his head, and his eyebrows drew together. "First of all, what movies have *you* been watching, young lady?" he teased, making a mockingly stern face and tightening his lips. Then his expression grew dark as he studied hers. "Secondly, that is total bullshit, and anyone who told you men don't like licking pussies..." He looked down, and the interest on his face was unmistakable. "Especially this exceptionally lovely little one..." He raised his eyes again. "Anyone who told you that was either an asshole or a liar—or probably both, given who I'm guessing might have said this."

Clothilde was shocked...but Marc didn't look as if he were lying. It was true that most of her information had come from a few dates with other generally self-centered society boys, and from Claude, who had not exactly turned out to be reliable.

"You mean you like...?" she trailed off, her cheeks heat again.

"Licking pussy?" Marc supplied, and his eyes gleamed. "I fucking love it, sweetheart, and I've been dreaming of tasting yours since the first time I saw you."

Clothilde was still hesitant, but the heat in Marc's eyes was undeniable. She wasn't sure if maybe he was just an exception, but his words were turning her on again when she'd thought she would be satiated for days.

"How about you open those soft thighs for me, let me pull off your panties, then you give me a chance to show you how much I like it. But if you're uncomfortable at all, we'll stop and we don't have to do it again?"

Clothilde nodded, just a slight incline of her head, really, but it seemed to be enough.

"Good girl," Marc praised in a low voice, and her nipples hardened again as a pulse of heat went straight to her empty channel. Everything this man did seemed to turn her on more than she'd known was possible.

He slid her panties down and off her legs quickly, as if he were afraid she'd change her mind, and dipped his head to kiss her wet folds.

At the first touch of his tongue, she moaned at the exquisite feeling. She started to close her thighs unconsciously, but he clamped his hands onto them to hold them open, and he proceeded to lick her from the bottom to the top of her slit, sucking lightly on the button of her clit and driving her absolutely wild. She screamed and thrashed her head back and forth on the bed, unsure whether she wanted to push toward him or away from him as the pleasure was so intense.

"You taste so good, baby…sweet and spicy, just like you," Marc said, his words ending in a sort of growl that she felt in vibrations of throughout her body. She reached her hands down to his short hair, barely resisting the urge to push him to the place he felt best. She was growing so wet that she could hear it as he sucked.

Marc chuckled. "I guess you like it, hm-m? Show me where you want me…where it feels best. I won't mind. I'll like it."

She wasn't sure if he meant it, because Claude had always gotten coldly angry at pretty much everything she'd done in bed, but she wasn't sure if she could stop herself, so she took him at his word and held Marc in place as he licked one spot that felt like heaven.

"Oh, *bon Dieu, putain*, right there...*oh là, oui*," she screamed in a mix of French and English. When he gently brushed the same spot with his finger and simultaneously thrust his tongue inside of her, something inside her just snapped and released and she soared into pure ecstasy, tightening her thighs around his head, her back bowing off the bed.

When she finally came back to herself, he was lazily licking her, and he still stroked her, using his fingers with exquisite gentleness as she tightened in periodic aftershocks.

"That was...incredible. I've... I didn't know it could be like that," she confessed, meaning it. "I don't even know if I could move right now. I feel like you just melted all my bones."

"You were amazing, trusting me like that." Marc smiled, but there was something strained in the expression. *Of course, dummy! You came twice, and he hasn't come at all*, she chided herself.

"Do you want me to, um, suck you?" she offered, feeling unaccountably shy saying it right out loud.

There was a soft rap on the door, and Marc swore under his breath.

"There had better fucking be a real emergency," he called, but the venom was muted, as if he were resigned to getting bad news.

"It's Menzies, sir...he, uh..."

It sounded like Barnes, and it was unlike him to beat around the bush. Clothilde had always been impressed by how forthright the young security officer was.

"Spit it out... I've heard it all," Marc said, sitting up and separating their bodies in a way that felt larger than just that moment...like he was putting a wall back up between them.

"He said that if you don't drag your ass away from, uh, the young lady — he used a different word — and get on the line in less than five minutes, you know the consequences."

The look he turned on Clothilde was agonized — and definitely guilty. A sick feeling started in the pit of her stomach. She'd thought they'd reached an understanding...however temporary. *Was I wrong yet again?* she asked herself. *Or did he realize that making love to me would be awful?*

"It's okay," she reassured him, pulling the blanket to cover her nudity, feeling suddenly vulnerable. "You can just come back after...whatever."

His expression was sad but determined. "No, Clo...it isn't fair to you. Whatever I want, we can't be...more. We shouldn't even be this — " He gestured between them. "Whatever we are now. You deserve better. I shouldn't stay with you. I shouldn't have done any of this. I was being selfish."

She wasn't certain if she heard much more beyond the refusal, and it felt as if he were wrenching her guts right out of her body. She went cold...to that icy place reserved for when Claude had been hurting her, in a rage. She'd sworn that she wouldn't ever allow herself to be this way again, but in spite of herself, her body and mind went blank, and she curled up under the blanket, refusing to look at Marc.

"Just go, then," she whispered. The soft snick of the door closing barely registered in her consciousness.

# Chapter Nine

Marc had hated a lot of the things he'd had to do as a soldier. He certainly hadn't always agreed with his orders, but he'd had to just grin and bear it, carrying out whatever was asked of him. There were sometimes impossible choices in impossible situations, and one of those choices had led to Cob's death. It had been agonizing, going to visit Cob's grandmother after his best friend had been killed. Even worse had been going to her funeral a scant month later because her heart had given out. He didn't believe that had been the reason she'd died…or it hadn't been only that. Her heart might have faltered, but it was because all hope of her baby grandson coming home had been extinguished.

That day — Cob's grandmother's funeral — had been the worst day of Marc's life. It wasn't because it hadn't been rough losing his own parents or Cob himself, but Granny Brown's passing had represented the death of Marc's belief in good in the world…that everything would turn out right in the end. He'd sworn vengeance.

More, he'd found a way to work with the US government to exact that vengeance. He hadn't cared about the cost. Whatever it was, he'd thought he'd be okay paying it. Just now, though, watching all the beauty that he'd shared with Clothilde fade and her icy exterior take back over, protecting her from her disappointment in him? That was a price he would never have wished to pay.

Unfortunately, he was trapped. Menzies had been giving him a coded warning, one confirmed by their brief conversation. His CO had mentioned again that the pressure about catching the Chimère at all costs wasn't coming from Menzies himself but somewhere higher — definitely somewhere more shadowy, with less accountability.

After the courtroom, Marc had already thought about their earlier discussion. If his conduct with Clothilde — and even a hesitation to come to the phone on a recorded, secure line would potentially be grounds enough for that — caused him to be found to be insubordinate, and likely also going AWOL, which he would be if he were officially disobeying direct orders with this trip, he would wind up in the obscure reaches of the military justice system.

He would go there, though, if it were only to save Clothilde pain. However, he wouldn't be going down alone. He thought of the younger operatives who followed him even now, and he also would be leaving Clothilde unprotected. Not only would she be without his security, but she'd be bait for someone else's trap. He couldn't allow that to happen.

He stood in the luxurious bathroom — *and why the hell are Luc Gaspard's bathrooms so fancy, even in the crew quarters for his damned ship?* — and stared in the mirror at the man he'd become. That guy was a real asshole. He'd needed to keep his distance from Clothilde Gaspard, who was not only the key to their investigation but a target of multiple attempts on her life. He just hadn't been able to do it, and he still wasn't sure why.

It wasn't as if he were only interested in sex, although he was still so fucking aroused from touching and tasting Clothilde that his cock was an iron bar in his pants, even after he'd jerked off furiously in the cold shower he'd just taken. It wasn't also only that he liked her, although he did. He had felt an instant sort of rapport with her from the first moment he'd seen her. He was fascinated by the way her mind worked, by the carefully guarded expressions that flitted across her face when she was amused or curious, when she first saw her family again after a little separation, when she saw *him*.

He sighed and lathered his face up, shaving almost on autopilot. He had changed into the sort of undercover uniform that he favored, dark pants with a dark sweater. They should be arriving soon, but his heart was no longer in any part of this mission except protecting Clothilde and the other guys.

"That's a good enough reason to fight for," he said out loud, and his reflection looked pretty damn determined, so he figured he must be, too.

When he stepped out of the bathroom, Brian Clark was waiting, and Marc wasn't surprised.

"Is Target Alpha awake?" Marc asked, deliberately using Clothilde's official code name to try to distance himself. After the harrowing evening she'd had, she should have slept longer, but he knew how difficult it was for her to sleep when she was concerned — not that it was his right or privilege to know that about her. *She would have slept better with you next to her*, a mental voice reminded him.

Clark cleared his throat uncomfortably, looking away.

"Yes, but she, ah, requested that she only see Barnes, Castellano and me."

It was a punch to the gut but not unexpected. Marc kept his face expressionless. "So, basically, *not* me. Got it."

"That's why I wanted to come find you, sir. I've been on this mission for a long time now—"

"Nobody could question your dedication, Clark," Marc agreed, cutting him off.

The younger man nodded. "Thank you, sir. That's what I mean, though. Did you know that Clothilde—I mean, Target Alpha—came to see me in the hospital several times?"

"She's a kind lady," Marc agreed in a curt tone.

"She's more than kind..." He cleared his throat. "Permission to speak freely?" Clark's expression was earnest and concerned, and Marc hated that his reputation had pulled in younger, talented soldiers like the three who currently manned the ship.

"Permission granted, unwillingly. But I know you're gonna say what you came to say."

"Thank you." Clark nodded. "She flew my momma in to visit me on the Gaspard private jet, and she called all my sisters personally. She said she wanted to thank them for my bravery. She didn't have to do that."

Marc hadn't known, but it sounded like something Clothilde would do. And he had just hurt her badly, again.

"That was very thoughtful of her," he answered.

Clark shook his head. "Barnes and I have seen the way you look at her and the way she looks at you, and what we can't figure out is why you don't just apologize. I'm not married." His mouth tightened, as if in regret, but only for an instant. "However, I do have three older sisters, and I've found that a well-placed apology goes a long way. Truth is, when I'm at home, I don't even mind apologizin' for things that aren't my fault, because it makes 'em all so happy."

The faces of any of the brave men and women who made it to his current, secretive unit were generally too grim to reveal much, but as much as it was possible, Clark's expression grew wistful. "If I had a woman like Clothilde Gaspard looking at me that way she looks at you, like she's starvin' and you're the last biscuit, I would never let an hour go by with her angry or hurt, and right now, she seems pretty damn furious and miserable."

"I'd be pissed if I didn't think you were really talking about someone else. What happened with your girl?" Marc probed.

Clark looked away. "I...don't know if I'll ever find out, but I regret it every day." As if recalling himself, he snapped his head back forward. "That's kinda my point, though. Remorse is an awfully shitty companion in bed at night."

Marc wanted to be mad, but the younger man, who had risked his life and almost died protecting Marina and Clothilde from Claude de Voltin, was so freaking earnest that it would be like kicking a puppy. Marc felt suddenly ancient.

"It's complicated," he answered simply.

"I'm sure it is," Clark acknowledged. "The thing about life is, even the complicated things are really simple when you break 'em down. I would do just about anything to protect and care for the people I love, and I think that's the kind of man you are, too. So Barnes and I just wanted you to know — Castellano, too — that whatever you need to do to protect her, that's fine with us. Even something crazy…like taking down the Chimère ourselves."

Marc's chin snapped up. *Holy shit. How have I not seen the best solution staring me in the face?* And yet, he had to put his men first. "It could mean a real shitstorm from high up…maybe even a closed-door military trial." That was part of what he'd wanted to protect the younger men from.

"We gathered that," Clark answered, his voice quiet but firm.

When Marc looked at Clark again, he didn't see just the young, dedicated soldier. He saw himself — the way he had been when he and Cob had first joined up, when they'd set out on their first overseas mission to save those who needed saving, help and save those weaker than themselves. It was time to make sure he was acting the way he should — the way *that* young man would, whether Clothilde could forgive him or not.

He put his hand on the younger man's shoulder and squeezed. "I'm honored, Brian. Thank you."

Clark nodded, his face impassive, but his eyes were proud.

"If she's up for it, you and Barnes should go over every guest with Clothilde in detail. Anything she can remember — anything at all — could be the key." Marc had intended to do that himself, but…well, the important thing was now that they find the Chimère as quickly as possible, no matter what.

"Understood." Clark nodded, and it was clear that he barely stopped himself from saluting.

"You do know we're totally screwed, right?" Marc felt compelled to add.

Brian Clark's expression grew a little feral, and Marc could see how he'd earned his fierce reputation.

"I say, bring it on."

*Yep. There's a good damn reason we all ended up in a top-secret special branch of Spec Ops.* Marc grinned. "Well, all right then."

The sun was rising as he stepped out onto the deck, and he could see the lonely rock island ahead of them, bathed in every shade between pink, purple, red and orange. Marc was reminded of his own description of Clothilde finding her pleasure, and he thought he might never see another sunrise without thinking of her.

The decommissioned lighthouse—with island—owned by the Gaspard family had limited cover, which was both an advantage and a liability. They'd be able to see anyone coming from a great distance, but even with the upgrades his team had recently made, just as a back-up, they were still somewhat more exposed than he'd like. Still, the whole thing was basically a fortress.

*Anyone who manages to follow us is in for a big, fucking surprise.* Marc's chest expanded with protective fury at the idea of someone coming here to try to hurt Clothilde, and he balled his hands into fists so tightly that his bones cracked. *Bring it on, indeed.*

\* \* \* \*

The antiseptic smell was overwhelming. Somehow, even in her dream, the hospital scent still practically singed the inside of her nose. Wait! Was she dreaming? Or...*remembering*?

The features around her were fuzzy and gray, but unmistakable. She'd seen them before. She was returning to a memory in a dream. Marc clutched her to his chest as he ran with her through some sort of... What was it? When she looked around, whimpering at the pain in her body, concentrated on her side, she saw stern men and women in a variety of military uniforms along with staff in medical scrubs.

*"Where's the bed for her?"* Marc had growled.

*"We can put her on a gurney, sir,"* one of the young-looking women who was obviously a nurse had offered.

*"No,"* he'd barked. *"I'll hold her until you have what you need."*

Another scrubs-clad man had approached at a clip so fast it was almost a run, but not quite. *Oh, that's right,* she'd thought fuzzily. *You're not supposed to run in hospitals. It scares the patients.* Still, with how fast the doctor or nurse was moving, she had still been a bit frightened.

*"Major Besson has arranged the custom drip in IC9 with the additional meds you advised would counteract the, uh,* RK781," he'd advised, dropping his voice on the last word, not even winded by his speed. Marc had turned on his heel to follow him, presumably to room IC9. *That doctor must be really fit,* she'd thought, and wondered how it was possible to be in so much pain but still feel kinda...blissed out. *Probably the world-rocking orgasm Marc gave me in the car. Wait! What?*

She must have made some sort of sound because Marc had looked down at her, although she'd only been able to see the stubborn lines of his chin above her.

*"Can you hear me, baby? God, I'm sorry…so sorry,"* he'd whispered under his breath as he'd rushed through the gleaming hallway, his voice low so she'd been sure only she could hear him. *"No matter what, I swear I'll take care of you, whatever it takes, but if this doesn't work – "* His voice had cracked, and the anguish in his words had been profound. *"I will follow whoever did this to the fucking ends of the earth to make them suffer. You're my every star, sweetheart…so bright I feel your light right into my bones."*

When she cracked her eyes open, the sun was sinking low in the sky, and Clothilde had a moment of confusion. Instead of hospital, now she smelled the salty air, which meant she was probably on Luc's ship—but no, she heard the instantly recognizable sound of waves crashing onto the rocky cliffs outside, and she didn't feel the telltale roll of a boat's movement. *Did I go to Grasse with Luc after all?* It felt too cold for the South of France, though…the air on her skin gave more of an impression of the North Atlantic.

She bolted upright in bed, the events of the previous night flooding back to her memory in a rush. They were at Wilson's Rock, the island and lighthouse her family owned off the coast of Northern Maine. Marc had taken her there because—according to Tim Barnes—it had been converted over the past couple of months into some sort of high-tech fortress. Being on the run from an unknown threat who was willing to shoot at her in the middle of a crowded city was crazy enough, but her dream came back to her, too, and suddenly all the strange flashes of memory made sense. It was no dream…and Marc Constantin had some serious explaining to do, *bordel.*

She found him in the first room she checked, the study — *typical* — which he'd converted to some kind of command center. His face, which she couldn't believe she'd once found stern and unreadable, registered surprise, then pleasure and finally wariness. She fought a spark of warmth at the knowledge that he'd been pleased to see her. She wasn't numb anymore, and she was working up to a towering rage.

"Really glad you got some rest, Duchess," he said by way of greeting, looking down again at the bank of monitors that now lined one of the walls of the room. Even with what had to have been intense renovations, she swore she could still smell the faint scent of her father's pipe smoke clinging to the leather of the chairs in three of the corners, which had remained the same since her childhood…probably since her father's childhood, too.

"I must have slept deeply because I had the strangest dreams."

She had studied him closely enough to recognize that Marc tensed, even though his posture remained outwardly relaxed.

"Oh?" he answered. "Will you be too cold if I we open a couple of windows?" As he gestured at her, she realized she still wore the baggy gym shorts and T-shirt she'd hurriedly taken from one of Luc's drawers on the ship. Still, *non sequitur* much?

"I should be fine," she replied, with no little amount of heat. "I'm used to the cold. Haven't you heard that they call me the Ice Queen?" She put her hands on her hips. "I think you'd be interested to hear what I dreamed about."

When she opened her mouth to continue, he pressed one rough palm to her lips, and she squeaked with indignation. He held his finger to his lips and mouthed, "One second," before going to open the windows.

She glared at him, pressing her lips together so tightly that they ached, but she obeyed his command. With both windows open, the sound of the rough surf and high wind filled the room, riffling any loose papers. Wordlessly, Marc gestured for her to join him at the window.

She almost refused, but even furious with him, she couldn't find it in her to discount what he obviously wanted.

"*Que diable*, Marc?" she hissed.

"Sorry, sweetheart. We swept the room, but I'm still not confident it's totally secure. The sound of the waves should help block devices from getting a clear recording or transmission. I want to be sure we can really talk."

Well, it sounded paranoid, but if what she suspected was true...it made sense. But Clothilde was still pissed off enough to bristle. "*Un*, you don't get to call me 'sweetheart'...or anything else besides 'Mademoiselle Gaspard'." She leaned closer, and she could smell a trace of deodorant and coffee. Marc looked tired, and she realized that he probably hadn't slept at all. She almost softened, but then reminded herself why she'd come storming down here in the first place. "*Deux*, I'm not sure I can believe you since you lied to me. I didn't have an allergic reaction all those months ago, did I? You took me to a military hospital for exposure to something, *conard*! How *dare* you lie to me about that!"

"Clo—"

She narrowed her eyes at him.

"I'm not calling you 'Mademoiselle Gaspard'," he said. "It seems ridiculous, since I had my head between your thighs less than twenty-four hours ago."

Clothilde stiffened. "That has nothing to do with this conversation, and I refuse to think about it."

Marc gave a sad half-smile. "And here I can't *stop* thinking about it, since it was probably the most glorious experience of my life."

"*Arrêtes!*" she said, holding up her hand as if to physically block him. "How the hell can I believe anything you say when you've obviously been lying to me all along?" She hated that her voice had a little quaver in it. "I mean, are you even a security guard?" The suspicion, which had been percolating since Annelise had mentioned it at the café, seemed to give voice to itself almost without her control. "Are you still somehow working for the military? On a mission now with my family?"

His face was carefully blank, and she raised both hands to his chest, pushing firmly. The move surprised her, and it obviously surprised him too, since he stumbled back a step. She jabbed her finger at his chest.

"I deserve the truth, Marc. Since my 'allergic reaction' was apparently an attack, then I've almost been killed *four* times now, and last night Claude *couldn't* have been involved since he's been totally locked down in custody. Now I realize that you had to have been expecting something like this, or you wouldn't have set this whole island up as a safe house...*after Claude was already arrested*." As she spoke, the pieces clicked together in her mind. "And Pierre must already know, too, or he would never have given you approval, *espèce de salaud*. If I don't know everything — or if you don't at least tell me *something* —

I'm in even greater danger if I'm not expecting a threat." The magnitude of the deception and betrayal, for both Marc and Pierre to have lied to her for so long, cut her to the quick so that she had to take a few steadying breaths as her eyes stung with tears she refused to acknowledge.

The emotion in his eyes was unexpected...a seeming combination of pride, respect and frustration. He raised his hand to cover hers where she still poked him, and the gesture was curiously tender.

"My whole adult life has been about honor," he started.

Clothilde wanted to object to the apparent change in subject, but something in the almost-sad set of his posture stopped her. She waited.

"If I go against my orders — *legal* orders — there will be serious repercussions."

Clothilde sucked in a harsh breath. She'd been anticipating the confirmation that he was still in the military, on a mission, and had been lying the whole time he'd been working for her family. Now that he'd basically agreed, though, without actually saying it, her rage began to drain out of her.

Marc held her gaze with his own and he looked agonized, torn apart. In that moment, she realized something important. She was asking him for everything, to give up his identity as a soldier and a hero, and he looked like he just might do it...for *her*. This man, who had helped her through her recovery from her accident and saved her life three more times since then, willing to sacrifice his own life in the process...held honor and duty at the core of his being. He was a hero, not only because of his prior actions, but in the way he was willing to make the difficult choices, to hold steadfast in the face of extreme pressure. *That* was the man she'd grown to care for, something woven into the fabric of him. She knew what she had to do.

When he started to speak again, she mimicked his earlier gesture and held her hand over his mouth. His eyes were surprised, questioning.

"I went to a very fancy boarding school. Did you know that?" She continued as if he hadn't been prevented from answering by her hand. "It was in New Hampshire, the campus full of pretty red brick buildings, complete with ivy crawling up the walls. I hated it at first, because it felt like Pierre and Rémy just didn't want me around anymore. Of course, now I realize that they were just doing their best, and they didn't have time to run the company and raise me full-time, but back then, I was lonely, hurting and poised to rebel." She gave a sad smile for the angry young teenager she'd once been. Marc gently caressed the back of her hand.

"I would have done it, too, if it hadn't been for my English teacher, Mrs. Westbroke. The other kids said she was close to a hundred, but I think she was probably in her early seventies. She introduced me to poetry...but more, she made me appreciate how the greatest stories, plays and poems have always helped people understand the complexities of human emotions, challenges...*la vie*, really." She paused, thinking of the diminutive teacher. "Mrs. Westbroke always wore a proper tweed suit, sensible low-heeled shoes and a tidy, white bun. She eschewed makeup, smelled like lily-of-the-valley and always drank exactly one glass of champagne or wine at events and parties." She could practically hear her former teacher's well-modulated voice, with the kind of New England accent that was most associated with the Kennedy family. She felt Marc's smile under her hand, but she didn't remove it.

"Do you want to know what Mrs. Westbroke's favorite poem was?"

Marc nodded slowly, never taking his eyes from hers.

"'To Lucasta, Going to the Wars', by Richard Lovelace. There's this one line that I have never forgotten, 'I could not love thee, dear, so much, lov'd I not honor more.' I thought of it the first time you and I met, in fact…and I just thought of it again." She finally lowered her hand from his mouth. "I care deeply for the man you are, and I'm not going to ask you to change that about yourself."

Marc held her gaze for a long moment, and the sound of the waves roared, echoing against the wood-paneled walls. He looked hard, like the elite military man and hero he still was, and probably always would be, no matter what his active-duty status was. He took the hand that she'd been holding against his lips and placed it back into the same position, kissing her palm tenderly before he lowered it again.

"Pretty sure I don't deserve that…or you." He stepped closer, so their bodies were nearly touching, and she could feel the heat of his skin under his plain, dark sweater. "I am truly sorry, though, Clothilde. I hate the way my actions have made you feel, and I'm determined to change, if it isn't too late."

As she looked at his tired face, the lines of it craggy from exhaustion, she felt time almost slow. His expression was full of remorse, but his eyes held something much deeper…something that echoed her own emotions. The sudden knowledge that she loved this man, had loved him for a long time, hit her so hard that she almost staggered.

She'd told him that she was okay with not knowing things, she'd recognized that she wouldn't love him the same — couldn't love him nearly so much — if he didn't possess such a laser focus on duty. Being a hero was part of the fabric of him. She just hadn't been willing to actually deal with the implications of it...the reality of what it felt like to come apart in his arms, then have him need to leave and apparently keep his distance because of his orders. She was ready now.

"You don't know how you've made me feel," she answered.

He raised his eyebrows, and something akin to hope warmed the blue of his eyes.

"Is that right, sweetheart?" He closed the distance between them so that their bodies were actually touching, front-to-front, and her nipples hardened against his chest. "You'd better tell me, then."

"How about I show you instead?"

# Chapter Ten

Marc had expected to have to seek Clothilde out, to apologize for fucking up with her, again. Both her appearance in the study and the revelation that she'd remembered everything from the night she was poisoned had shocked the hell out of him. More astonishing, though, had been her understanding. He didn't think another woman in a million could ever have understood his position and given him license to do what he needed to do. It made something inside him that was coiled up and heavy, weighing his every move and thought, relax.

He'd already decided that he would push the boundaries of the asinine order that he keep his distance from her while getting close, and he would go beyond the scope of his orders to bring in the Chimère and end this, once and for all. Now that Clothilde remembered everything else that he'd been trying to avoid, it seemed pointless to continue to hide the rest, too. If he were headed to being taken off the op anyway, then he had better make damn sure that he resolved everything as quickly as fucking possible, because there was no way he was leaving Clothilde again—not now, not ever. He sure as hell wasn't letting her be locked up in some military prison, even for protection. He wasn't sure he ever could have done that.

This—the reality of her full knowledge and understanding in spite of it...*because* of it—was better than he'd ever imagined. He cared for her too much not to make her understand their position, though.

"Duchess...my God, you don't know how much I want you to do that," he said in a voice strangled at the end as she shifted slightly against him, her soft curves caressing him from chest to hips.

"I think I might have an idea," she teased.

He loved seeing her like this, and he marveled that, after so much pain in her past, she could still manage to be so open and giving—especially with him. It wouldn't be right to go any further, though—*not this time*—without giving her the full picture.

He sighed. "You remembering what you have, it changes everything—and now, no matter what..."

He stumbled over the words when he saw the hope burning in her eyes. If he could have saved this one moment forever, to take out and look at again if he was eventually—*probably*—caged in some remote military prison cell, he would have bottled it in an instant.

"No matter what, I'll be gone." There. He'd said it as nicely as he could.

She froze. "What do you mean 'gone'?"

He frowned, already hating that her expression had changed to worry instead of hope. The warmth was still there, though.

"Gone...as in, I will disappear. It won't change the way I feel, or that I'm gonna do everything I can to protect you as long as this scarred-up carcass of mine lets me, but at some point, sooner or later, that'll be it, and I just don't want you to have any regrets — any *more* regrets — about anything we do."

Her eyes looked like liquid velvet in the soft light of the setting sun. Clothilde Gaspard didn't need the light of the golden hour of dusk to look stunning, but the additional gilding from it was making her look practically ethereal, like a goddamn angel.

He was so lost in her, and it almost surprised him when she spoke.

"First, I regret many things, but...caring for you will never be one of them."

Had she been about to say something else? He was pretty sure he didn't deserve to hope for that.

"Second, how could your government ever let that happen?" she continued.

He gave a snort that could have been a laugh if it hadn't been so humorless.

"*Let* that happen? Baby, they would be the ones *making* it happen."

She looked first confused, then appalled.

"How do you think things end for men like me when we've outlived our usefulness? Or when the risk of what we know outweighs other considerations?"

The sound of the sharp breath that she sucked in cut through even the ongoing roar of the rough surf on the rocks.

"How could you sign up for this? You *can't* be okay with it!"

For a woman who was reported to be so haughty and worldly, Clothilde still possessed a core of solid kindness and surprising innocence about certain things. Marc fucking loved that about her. In fact, with uncomfortable clarity, he realized he loved just about everything about her. *I love her, full stop.* Damned inconvenient time to recognize it, when he was trying to make peace with what would inevitably be their short future together, one way or another.

"Are you saying you're *fine* with it?" she reiterated her question, and he shook his head, bringing his attention back to her.

"I wouldn't say I was fine with it, but I knew the risks. I just… Let's just say I thought it was worth it. I'm, ah, *less* fine with it now."

She looked up at him, so lovely, inside and out, that it made his heart stutter.

"What changed?" she whispered.

He lifted his right hand to cup her cheek, sweeping his thumb across her silky skin. "I met you," he answered simply.

She pushed up onto her tiptoes to press her lips to his. At the touch of her mouth, it felt as if something that had been holding him back snapped inside of him, filling him with an aching longing. She might have started the kiss, but he took it over, wrapping his arms around her lithe form, softly curved in all the right places. He ravaged her with his mouth, savoring the taste of her that he'd thought never to sample again. Her hair smelled faintly of a different shampoo—she must have taken a shower before sleeping—and it felt soft against his palm as he cupped the back of her, stroking his other hand up and down the silky skin of her back, bare under the baggy T-shirt she wore.

She moaned and twined her arms around his neck, trying to pull him closer—as if he could get any closer without being inside her. He nibbled her lips, then pushed his tongue inside to caress hers. She gave a little mewl of pleasure and rocked her hips against his, making him gasp as she connected with the hard ridge of his cock. It had been semi-hard since she'd walked in—all she had to do was look or breathe in his direction, and it stood right at attention—but now it grew so full it was nearly uncomfortable.

He reached down to palm the soft globes of her ass and, when she threw her head back with a moan, he hitched his hands under her, lifting her against him and walking them toward the nearest wall. She wrapped her bare legs around his waist, and he rubbed against her with every small movement of his hips, pressing her into the cool stone of the original lighthouse wall. She was practically panting, her head thrashing from side to side, as he licked and kissed each side of her neck in turn.

"Marc, oh, Marc," she murmured, her tone a mix of passion and tenderness.

The sound of his name on her lips recalled him slightly, and he realized he had Clothilde pressed hard against a cold, rock wall—his Clothilde, with her soft skin that showed marks easily, and her hip and leg that still ached more than she would ever admit. He stopped moving and buried his face in her neck, trying to slow his breathing.

"I'm sorry...shit, baby, I'm sorry I got so carried away," he mumbled.

"I'm not," she breathed, and he snapped his head up to look at her.

Her eyes were bright with desire and something deeper...infinitely warmer. She took his face in between her hands. He knew he wasn't much to look at, just a somewhat ordinary collection of features, maybe a little too harsh, although he did take care to keep his body in top condition for his work. The way Clothilde looked at him, though — the way she was looking at him now — the frank appreciation and affection in her gaze nearly made him want to blush. *Goddamn, my Ice Queen is fiery.*

"You can touch me however you want to, Marc, and I am never going to regret it," she continued in a soft but certain voice, and it was both a statement and promise.

His cock swelled impossibly harder, longer, throbbing where it still pressed against her and an unreasoning rush of pure, masculine pride filled him, making him want to puff out his chest and give a whoop of joy. Still, he wanted to be sure. She was too precious to him not to be.

"You're certain? Even knowing what might — probably will — happen?" he asked.

Her small smile was both sad and sexy as hell. "*Oui. I want all of you that I can have, mon amant...mon amour.*"

Her words seemed to unleash something in him, and he kissed her as if he wanted to devour her, to possess her entirely. She was so caught up — practically drugged — in the pleasure of his kisses that she barely realized when he lifted her again, never separating their mouths, and carried her to the enormous brown leather sofa that had been in the study for as long as she could remember. The leather was cool on her bare skin as he laid her along the length of it, but she warmed up again nearly instantly as he stretched out on top of her.

When Claude had taken control, she'd been afraid — and she'd had good reason to be — never knowing what he would do next or when he would turn mean. During the last year or so of their relationship, he had pretty much always switched over to random cruelty at some point. With Marc, though, she *loved* the way he took control. She wanted to be at his mercy, loving the anticipation of him bringing her pleasure. In spite of the lies between them, which she could understand weren't his choice, she still trusted him with her body — and with her heart.

She let her thighs fall open and looped her arms back around him as well, an invitation for him to fit himself against her. He obviously understood, settling his weight on top of her with a grunt of satisfaction.

"God, you feel so good, baby," he groaned, flexing his hips so his sex rubbed against hers, even through the fabric of their clothes.

He felt enormous, and she had a moment of trepidation, wondering how much it might hurt if she wasn't wet enough, but she forced herself to remember that this was Marc…nobody else. Marc had proven that he would never hurt her. He must have sensed her tension, though.

"We can go really slow, sweetheart, or you can change your mind. Just let me know. I want everything we do to feel good to you."

It was so sweet and so characteristically thoughtful of the tough-looking soldier that she ached. It banished any remnants of fear, reminding her that, even before she'd known how he felt about her, she had trusted and turned to this man — dreaming of and pining for him when they were apart. They were both here, now, in this one moment, and she was not losing out on having all she could of him.

"I'm okay," she confirmed. "I love the way you feel...but, well, I'm fine with going slow."

Marc smiled above her, the expression purely tender. His form was silhouetted by the last, dying rays of the sunset, so that he looked like a blend of light and shadow, like the man himself.

"It will be my great pleasure to take my time with you, Duchess." His voice was like gravel, sexy and rough, and she gave a little shiver. "Mm-m," he whispered, leaning down to nip at her earlobe. "I guess you like that idea."

"Yes," she breathed.

"I can feel your hard little nipples just begging for some attention," he continued.

She could feel them, too, tight and aching, rubbing against the hard planes of his chest. She arched her back, almost in spite of herself, and he gave a dark chuckle.

"Oh yeah, let's get these clothes off you so I can show them I haven't forgotten about them." His sexy teasing was just what she needed, making her smile and defusing her sudden nervousness.

She lifted at his urging, allowing him to pull her shirt up over her head before he slid the large, borrowed shorts down and off her legs, leaving her nude on the dark leather while he knelt on the floor. His look of deep appreciation and naked lust warmed her and made her want to squirm with the sudden heat in her core.

"Fucking gorgeous." He pressed one hand to his chest. "You take my breath."

She flushed with pleasure at the outrageous compliment.

"*Menteur, mais je l'aime,*" she said in French, knowing that he would understand. *Liar, but I like it.* In fact, he likely spoke more languages than she did.

"I'm nothing special, baby," Marc answered, but he reached for the hem of his thin sweater, pulling it up and over his head from the bottom.

She placed her hand onto his newly bared chest, which was so warm it practically radiated heat. The crinkly blond hairs that covered it were surprisingly soft.

"You're something special to me, Marc," she answered, and with a groan, he leaned forward to claim her mouth again.

She'd thought he'd been passionate and commanding before, but now she realized that he must have been holding back, as he began a full-on sensual onslaught. He plundered her mouth with his while he roamed his hands everywhere, stroking, teasing, arousing—sometimes rough, at other times barely there. She became nearly mindless with need, crying out and thrusting her hips up, touching him in return everywhere she could reach. His fresh, outdoor scent surrounded her, so that she filled her lungs with Marc with every ragged breath.

When he plucked at her nipples, she arched her back so much she nearly levitated off the couch, and he chuckled against her lips.

"Clo, those fucking sexy nipples of yours are going to make me shoot off before I'm ready if I'm not careful," he murmured. "I think they ought to be punished." Goosebumps rose all over her arms and chest at his words, and his grin was feral. "Oh, yeah, you like that idea, don't you?"

She nodded, shocked to realize that she really did.

Marc took one nipple into the hot cavern of his mouth, making her breathless. When he nipped gently at her with his teeth, though, she went almost dizzy with arousal.

"Unh...*oh, là*..." She made a sort of mixture of incoherent sounds in French and English, but Marc seemed to understand. He swirled his tongue around and around each nipple, sucking, then punctuating the attention with a small bite. She thrashed and screamed, wild with pleasure, and her channel went liquid with need until she was desperate with emptiness.

"Marc!" she whimpered, and he finally took pity on her.

"Have they been punished enough, then?" he asked. "Do you know, sweetheart, I think that your pretty little pussy might need to punished, too? What do you think?"

"Please...oh, please," she whispered.

She was so aroused, her folds swollen from his attentions to her breasts, that when his fingers found her little bundle of nerves, his touch set off a shockwave of bliss almost instantly. He swallowed her hoarse yell with his kiss, stroking her and drawing out her pleasure with exquisite gentleness until the last quakes subsided.

Breathless, and so sweaty that her skin was sticking to the shiny leather of the couch, she went limp, totally spent. The room had gone darker, so that only Marc's eyes glittered. She would have been upset at how smug he seemed except she felt too damn good.

She was overcome by a wave of tenderness and the need to give him pleasure, too. He'd been so good to her. In fact, she didn't think she'd ever felt anything like it. Everything seemed different with him...better. She knew what he must really want, though. In that moment, she longed to give it to him...no matter the cost. He was worth the pain.

"I changed my mind," she said, when she could breathe again.

"You did?" he answered, his voice wary.

"*Oui*...I can't take any more of your 'slow'. I'm not sure I'll survive it."

His bark of laughter was pure, masculine satisfaction.

"I'd like to prove you wrong—" he started, but she cut him off, deciding to be bold in spite of the unease in the pit of her stomach. She could do this for him.

"*Oh, non*...come inside me, *mon amour*... Come fill me now." She reached down to find his hardness with her hand and realized that he must have shucked off his pants and underwear at some point without her knowing. He felt huge, hot and incredibly hard as she circled him with her fingers, which barely fit around his girth.

"As my duchess commands," he said, his grin both cocky and predatory. "Let me go get a condom, and I can assure you that I'm clean, according to my regular required tests."

She shook her head, a small, jerky motion. "I'm on birth control, and I'm clean, too. Please, go ahead." She knew he probably heard the strain in her voice as eagerness, but she worried it was mostly fear. She wanted to get this part over with.

# Chapter Eleven

As he rose over her, she felt an instinctual inward cringe, suddenly worried at how much he could hurt her with his large size. All her prior confidence vanished, and she closed her eyes, bracing herself when she felt him poised at her entrance.

Instead of the familiar horrible stretching and scraping, so that she felt raw inside every time she'd agreed to make love to her ex-fiancé, Marc didn't enter her.

"What's wrong, sweetheart?" His accent was as thick as she'd ever heard it, and she saw no anger or frustration in his eyes, only concern.

"I... It's fine. Just do it. Go ahead." Her bravado seemed to ring hollow, but she hoped he couldn't hear it. Of course, he did.

"You're so tense that it might hurt you right now, Clo," he said gently, starting to pull back. She forced herself to open her thighs.

"I, ah, think I'm just made that way. It's always been like that, but I want this...want to give this to you." She gritted her teeth, not realizing she'd also closed her eyes until she opened them again when she still didn't feel him enter her. Marc looked thunderous, and she cringed.

"Oh, baby, I'm not angry with you. I just... I think I should have killed your asshole of an ex when I had the chance." He visibly took a calming breath. "Making love should be beautiful and pleasurable for everyone or it shouldn't happen."

"So...you don't want me anymore?" she asked in a small voice, feeling her eyes fill with unwanted tears and shifting under him to try to cover herself up.

"Oh no, Clo...never that. I want you so bad my fucking teeth hurt with it, always...but not like this. Whatever we do, I want you to enjoy the hell out of it." Stifling a wince, he eased himself off her, and she curled into a miserable ball.

She heard him cross the room, and the click of a lamp turning on. She could only see the dim increase in light from behind her eyelids, which she'd squeezed shut. A fleeting wish that she could just melt into the sofa and disappear passed through her mind.

She felt the soft fabric of a cashmere throw-blanket on her naked skin before Marc's weight settled back onto the couch next to her.

"C'mere, baby. I want to hold you." It wasn't a request so much as an order, but his voice was gentle. She didn't resist when he lifted her onto his lap, turning her face into his chest so that his hair tickled her nose.

They sat there in silence for a long moment. Marc was comfortable with quiet, maybe even more than speaking, she'd realized.

"I'm so embarrassed," she finally said, her face still muffled by his skin so she was afraid he wouldn't hear her over the continued loud sound of the surf. "I...should have told you that there is something wrong with me for, you know, making love."

Marc rubbed a soothing hand up and down her back under the blanket. She was grateful for its warmth since the warm day had turned to a cool night, and the room was breezy from the open windows.

"Is it always like that? You get tense?"

Clothilde flushed, feeling a wave of shyness to talk so frankly. "Yeah," she confirmed. "I'm sorry," she mumbled.

"Don't be sorry, baby. I'm not mad, and I'm not going anywhere. I just want to understand better." He tightened his arms. "Does it feel any different after you come a few times?" he prompted quietly.

Clothilde thought about it. She really hadn't done much deep reflection about it, since after Claude had cheated on her, the subject had been too painful. She'd been certain he'd gone elsewhere because she hadn't been able to give him what he wanted. Then, after it had become clear that he'd been attacking her family, she'd had to avoid thinking about him altogether or she felt awful for never realizing that someone she'd spent so much time with, someone she'd thought she loved, had been hiding his hatred and insanity.

Thinking back on their physical intimacy now, though, after having been with Marc...it gave her new perspective. "I'm...actually not sure if I ever, um, *came* with anyone else."

"Never?" He sounded surprised.

She shrugged, although it was tiny, pressed as she was against him. "I'm pretty certain, now, since it never felt anything like the way you made me feel."

"But did you kiss, rub, touch…other stuff to warm you up?"

Clothilde thought back again. "With some of my high school boyfriends, *oui*, but it never went too far. And Claude? He thought women should be cool and reserved."

"So he just, what? Shoved himself inside you?" Marc's growl held tightly leashed fury.

She nodded but hurried to explain. "He told me that I should always be wet, though…but I'm, well, *not*." It felt even worse than she'd expected, to confess it out loud.

"*Fuck,* baby."

She flinched at his tone.

"He was lying to you, that piece of shit. There's nothing wrong with you. That isn't how it should be. *Any* woman would react the same way. Your body and your mind have to be at least somewhat aroused. And lots of couples use lube, too." Every line of his body was tense underneath her, and she could feel the definition of his muscles everywhere. She lifted her head to look at Marc, and his expression was furious, his eyebrows drawn together and the muscle in his jaw twitching. "He was hurting you and telling you it was your fault. I fucking want to find him and rip his nails out, one by one."

Hope rose inside her that maybe she'd been wrong. *Bon Dieu*, she'd been wrong about so many other things relating to Claude. And yet… "But if you make me feel so good—and you really do—why is it still happening?"

Marc made a visible effort to relax and looked down at her. "I'm guessing because your body only associates penetration with pain, so it tenses on its own."

Her heart fell. "So there's nothing we can do about it?"

His eyes gleamed. "I didn't say that... I suspect there are a lot of things we can do about it." He shifted her so he could reach one of her nipples again. When he brushed over it with his thumb, she gasped. When he cupped her breast in his hands, her tension melted away, and arousal flooded back.

"Marc," she said, warning in her voice.

He continued to tease her until she was squirming on his lap, and she could feel his growing hardness, rising between her thighs.

"I don't have any lube here, but I could lick you again, too...and maybe really use my fingers inside you — not just the tip — just to get you more used to the idea."

"But what about you?" she panted. "I want it to be good for you."

His eyes gleamed in the soft, yellow light. "Oh, it's good for me to watch you." He spoke with such conviction that she couldn't doubt his sincerity. "But I didn't say you couldn't touch me or lick me...anywhere you want."

"But I want you inside of me. I've dreamed of it, so many times."

Marc gave a strangled sound, almost as if he were in pain. "God, baby...my *God*. When you say things like that...you're not messing around." His chest rose and fell like a bellows. "We can work up to that...after you're okay with my fingers, then we can try having me put my cock into your sweet little pussy, inch by inch, so you can stop me if it's too much."

"Let's start right now, then," she said, emboldened by his words, the desire pulsing through her from his touch, and the urgency, knowing their time might be limited. She felt wild and reckless...but more alive than she had, well, *ever*.

"Shit, sweetheart...you're so fucking sexy." He closed his eyes, shaking his head as if to clear it. "We should have at least a day before we need to go on high alert. I'm supposed to take early watch, but I'll ask Clark if he can take it so we can have more time alone. You hold that thought... Hold it right in the front of your mind, all right?"

He tweaked her nipple once more as if to punctuate his words and she squeaked, moisture gushing to her core. Marc practically ran out of the room, only remembering to grab a second throw-blanket to wrap around himself at the last second.

Clark had gladly agreed to take the first overnight watch shift from Marc. Marc was impressed that the younger operative had almost managed not to look askance at the blanket Marc wore, toga-style. As Marc had walked away—well, hurried was a more apt description—Barnes had joined Clark and the two of them had poorly hidden snorts of laughter behind coughs. Frankly, Marc didn't care.

Clothilde had apparently been able to forgive him, which already made him the luckiest SOB around. On top of that, even knowing that he was pretty much doomed—and he really couldn't dwell on that too much at the moment—she wanted to make some sweet memories with him. If he only did two more things before he died, making love to Clothilde was on the top of the list and catching the Chimère to avenge Cob's death as well as the attacks on Clothilde and her family was second. Being with her, after believing it was impossible for so long, was almost unimaginable. Of course, he'd almost fucked it up entirely less than twenty-four hours earlier and was likely to fuck it up again, soon…hence, he was hurrying like a reject from a Greek fraternity party, unashamed, in front of his subordinate officers.

He half-expected her to have changed her mind when he got back to the study, but she still sat on the couch, wrapped in the blanket he'd put on her. He took that as, if not confirmation, then a good sign. She stood when he entered, so beautiful that it felt surreal to be here, alone, in such an intimate setting with her.

"*Tout rangé*, then?" Her smile was tentative as she asked him if all was arranged.

He'd noticed that she slipped into French more frequently with him, seemingly unconsciously, and it warmed him since she usually only forgot with her family. His Clothilde was clever, realizing relatively early on that even though his accent sucked, he spoke and understood quite fluently, thanks to his late French-Canadian grandfather.

"I'm all yours, at least for the next few hours," he answered.

"I was thinking…"

He braced himself. She'd changed her mind. He understood. He'd played with her emotions one too many times, and she'd obviously been hurt more deeply than anyone had realized by her relationship with Claude de Voltin. She surprised him.

"Have you been up into the tower?"

He cocked his head. "No, actually, I haven't. We put some cameras up there, of course, and even a noise muffling device that only works for smaller spaces, but I've been staying where the walls are thicker in the rest of the house."

Her smile was a secretive half-moon, and he loved it.

"Come with me?" He must have hesitated because she paused. "Unless it isn't safe?"

He considered it. Their position would be more exposed up there, sure, but part of the reason they'd come to Wilson's Rock was the incredible visibility. Hell, they'd even installed external underwater sensors to alert them of incoming submarines. He truly didn't anticipate any sort of attack this soon, although he certainly expected one within the next few days.

"No, we should be safe. I'll follow your lead, Duchess," he answered, and he knew by the sudden spark in her eyes that she knew he wasn't talking only about the tower. *Interesting*.

The stairway was narrow, winding and cold, even in midsummer, because of the thick stone. In fact, the whole island was chillier than the mainland, since it was set out a little way from the nearest shore, exposed to the ocean winds. Each step had a shallow dip worn into it, from over a hundred fifty years of other feet walking up, touching the exact same spot. Marc was concentrating so hard on the gentle sway of Clothilde's lush ass underneath her thin blanket—and damn, she had a gorgeous ass...round, soft, and surprisingly curvy for her statuesque frame—that he didn't immediately realize they'd reached the lantern room.

When he did look up, the beauty of the surroundings made his jaw fall open. The space was round, every wall a window, and the old beacon was still preserved in the center, as well as the domed cupola above. The rest of the décor had been totally changed, though, with brightly colored wide window seats added all around, their fabric a variety of soft-looking velvets. The round room had obviously been enlarged, but somehow the integrity of the original tower remained. Beyond the gorgeous interior, though, the view was absolutely magnificent. It felt almost as if they were a part of the stars themselves.

"Do you like it?" she asked, and something about the tone of her voice made him think it was more than just an idle question.

"It's amazing, Clo. I've never seen anything like it." He meant the words wholeheartedly, but he would have lied his ass off to see the glow of pleasure on her face.

"I talked Pierre into letting me remodel it myself when I was still in school. I used to come up here whenever I could to get some peace. Obviously, we don't get guests very often…"

He chuckled. "Not exactly city center," he agreed.

The expression on her face was almost a smile, but it was too sad to have been called that. "I don't remember as much about our mother as Pierre and Rémy do, but I do recall that she loved the water, and she thought having her own island, complete with lighthouse, was just *fantastique*." She pursed her lips. "I sometimes have wondered if Luc remembers the same thing, and that's why he loves his boat so much." She walked to one of the window seats, looking out. "I might have started coming here as a way to be closer to her, but renovating this room made it *mine*."

Marc could see that—could see a lot more than she probably wanted him to, in fact. "You are not at all what people think."

She sat down on the edge of the seat. "*Non*," she agreed simply. "I am not."

"Thank you for showing me," he said.

"The view is better sitting on one of the seats," she offered.

He sat down next to her, so close that his thigh brushed against hers. She was right that the view was spectacular, even better from the seat, but he couldn't take his eyes off her face.

"Much better," he agreed, staring at her blanket, which threatened to slip down her shoulder.

She saw where he was looking and laughed.

"I like you like this," she said.

"Nearly naked?" he suggested, waggling his eyebrows. Her peal of laughter echoed against the glass walls, like a bell.

"Well, yes...I do like that. But I meant that you seem lighter right now. You're always so very serious, my Marc." She made a little moue with her lips, and he wanted to kiss her, so he did, a fleeting kiss before he pulled back.

"Being with you has always made me feel lighter, I suppose," Marc answered.

"Were you like this all the time, once?" she guessed.

He thought about it for a moment. "You know, I was always a serious kid...grew up poor and tough. My parents died young, violently, and growing up in the foster care system was...difficult, to put it mildly. But Cob—he was my best friend, from the same neighborhood—he always made me laugh. We joked a lot together and got into a shitload of trouble with our pranks, too."

The adorable little crinkle appeared on her forehead. "Cob? I think this is the first time you've mentioned him."

He knew it was. "I don't...I stopped talking about him, after he was killed."

She sidled even closer to him, draping her legs over his lap, and taking one of his hands in both of hers. "What happened to him?"

"It's classified...really, almost anything more than his name is classified."

"Ah," she said, understanding in her eyes. She really was probably too clever for her own good.

"I can tell you that much, though. His ma wanted him to have a grand name, something respectable, so she saddled him with Cornelius Ogilvy Brown. When he was little—although man, he was never *that* little—kids called him Corny. As he got older, and much, much bigger, we started calling him Cob, and it just stuck."

"I can tell from how you talk about him that you were close," she observed.

He nodded. "Like brothers, from when we were young, and even more so when we joined up together."

"I don't need to know how it happened to be very sorry that he died."

Marc squeezed her hand. "Thank you, sweetheart. He would have loved you."

They sat in silence for a couple of minutes, but there was nothing uncomfortable about it. He was content to hold her, to feel the warm weight of her legs on his lap.

Clothilde was the one to break the silence. "It feels right to have you here."

He looked at her questioningly and she continued.

"I was surprised when you told me we were headed here, of all places, but I'm happy to be here with you…to have you enjoy my secret place."

He tried to hold it in, knowing that she'd spoken seriously, but he just couldn't help himself. "I'd like to enjoy all your secret places, baby," he answered with a teasing leer, and she burst into laughter.

"Oh, *bon Dieu*, that was *horrible!*" She pronounced the word the French way, swatting him on the shoulder. "It seems so wrong to laugh right now."

"Naw, it's natural. We always crack the most jokes as we head to the very worst ops. It lets off tension," he reassured her.

"I can think of another way we could do that," she said, her voice going low and sultry. Just like that, his cock stiffened almost painfully, as if straining toward her. *Down, boy*, he told it. He'd promised Clothilde slow, and he was about to shoot off before he even got inside her. *Shit on a shingle*, he thought, mentally borrowing Menzies' favorite curse.

"Oh yeah?" he prompted. Her answering smile was wicked.

"Yeah…" She paused for effect, running one finger slowly down his chest so that goosebumps rose all over his skin. "I've heard yoga and meditation are wonderful."

He let out a full-on belly laugh at her teasing.

"That was very saucy, baby…but didn't anyone ever tell you not to poke the bear?"

She shook her head, making her hair shimmer in the light of the nearly full moon. This high up in the lamp room, with no light pollution from anywhere, it felt like they could have touched the moon and stars.

"Nope...nobody has ever told me that, and you are a bear that I would very much like to poke," she answered, then prodded him in the middle of his chest unrepentantly.

"I think you might have just earned yourself a punishment, young lady," he growled. He'd noticed before that she seemed to enjoy it when he was very commanding, and he saw the telltale flush rise on her cheeks again at his words.

"What kind of punishment?" she asked, sounding intrigued and breathless.

"I think you need to take off your blanket and open your legs so I can lick you again and see if you like having my fingers inside you."

"Oh, Marc," she responded, biting her lip. She looked excited, but nervous too. "What if... What if I can't?"

He made his tone stern. "Don't trust me, baby?"

Her answer was gratifyingly swift. "Oh, I do...with my life."

He shrugged. "Well, then...trust me that I won't make you uncomfortable, and you tell me if I ever do anything you don't like." He disentangled himself from her legs, letting his own blanket drop in the process as he stood, naked, with his manhood jutting up like an overeager new recruit.

She gulped at the sight of it.

"Are you going to do as you were told, or do I have to hold those creamy thighs open myself?"

Her eyes widened, and he could see her heartbeat quicken in the hollow of her throat. "I'll do it," she said, and undid the loose knot of her covering so it slithered down her form like a caress. Holding his gaze, she leaned back and let her legs part. She must have still been wet from his earlier attention because the petals of her sex were shiny in the pale light.

"Fucking spectacular," he breathed, and knelt on the floor in front of her, his knees cushioned by his blanket. "I thought I might never get to taste you again."

He lowered his head to her core and her flavor exploded into his mouth, tangy and sweet, indescribable and addictive. His cock bobbed and begged for attention, and he could feel the cooling drops of pre-cum that had seeped out onto the tip, but he told it to wait. *They* could wait. Making Clothilde comfortable again was of paramount importance. He began again with slow, leisurely kisses. He'd always like the taste of a woman's nectar, but lapping at Clothilde, feeling her thighs squeeze around him, hearing her breathy little mewls of pleasure and delight? It was something else entirely.

When she was slick with arousal, he knew she was ready.

"You're so wet, baby...such a good girl to get so creamy for your man. I'm gonna slip my fingers inside to make you feel so fucking good." He could practically sense her trepidation through her skin, warring with how turned on he knew she was. "You trust me to make you feel good, don't you? Anything you don't like, we stop right away."

She nodded, just a small nod, but it was enough.

He slowly worked first one finger, then a second into her. She resisted slightly at first, but when he hummed against the button of her clit, she gasped and opened up, allowing him to slide right in. She had grown so drenched that his fingers made a wet sound in the otherwise-silent room, and her breathing grew uneven, gasping.

Still, he circled her with his tongue, exquisitely gentle, even while he pumped his fingers into her deeper and deeper.

"Does that feel good, baby?" he ground out, wanting to hear her say it.

"*Bon Dieu, oui, oui,* yes," she answered in a broken voice. "Please, Marc, *je t'en supplie,*" she begged, and primitive satisfaction rose in his breast.

"I'm gonna add a third finger, now, because I want you to feel how good it can be to have something thicker...something like me." His cock jumped at his words and desire was like a wild thing in his gut, spreading everywhere, but he continued to ignore it, focusing on her.

"Oh, God, yes...Marc, *please,*" she urged.

She was so soaked by the time he thrust into her with three fingers that they slid right in, and she cried out, reaching out seemingly unconsciously to hold him closer.

"So good...feels so good," she moaned. He licked and sucked even faster and speared into her with his fingers, curling them up slightly toward himself until she screamed and convulsed all around him so that he couldn't breathe for a solid minute. He would have happily passed out, though, to see the look of wonderment on her face when he was finally able to look up at her again.

"You felt...oh, *bon Dieu,* that was amazing. Your fingers inside me..." She trailed off and her expression was dreamy, sated. He couldn't resist moving them ever so slightly, setting off a whole-body quake that made her breasts jiggle.

"You liked it?" he prompted, already knowing her answer and feeling unaccountably cocky.

"Oh, Marc," she sighed, then gasped as he finally pulled his fingers from her channel slowly. "It was...better than *anything*."

He couldn't keep the grin from his face. "I'll take your compliment, sweetheart, and what a compliment it is, but...I think it might be able to get even better."

Her eyes darkened and instead of an angel, she looked like one-hundred-percent vixen. "*Vraiment?*" she asked. *Truly?* "I want to feel you... Kiss you. *Now.*"

The shape of her lips as she spoke nearly made him come, and he worried he might just explode as soon as she so much as breathed on him, like a randy teenager in the backseat of a goddamn car, but he didn't care.

"You do anything you want to me, Duchess. Anything at all."

Clothilde reveled the in the powerful feeling Marc's words gave her. This man — huge, muscular, physically much stronger than she could ever hope to become — was willing to put himself at her mercy. She could sense that he preferred to give the orders, and she loved the way he did that, but in this moment, having him give her *carte blanche* to his body was exactly what she needed.

"Get up here, then, and let me touch you everywhere," she said in her most imperious Ice Queen voice, testing him. He looked bemused, but she didn't miss the flame of heat in his glacial blue eyes, either. He liked it when she was haughty.

He stood with more grace than she would have expected from such a muscle-bound man, but she'd seen before how stealthy he could be when he'd rescued her from Claude at the cabin in Vermont. *Because of his advanced training, of course, since he's still on a mission for some sort of special branch that he never told you about*, the nasty little voice in the back of her head reminded her, sounding suspiciously like her ex-fiancé. All her doubts fled, though, when she saw the tenderness in his expression. He was willing to tame himself for her.

He stretched out, naked, on the wide velvet seat in front of her. He was unabashed in his nudity. In fact, he practically preened, and she could have sworn he was making his muscles ripple on purpose. But of course, the man had nothing whatsoever to be self-conscious about. He was built like a Greek god. She drew her eyes down along every line of his body, drinking him in. This was the first time she was seeing him completely bare, she realized. *Oh là*, he was something, her Marc.

A flurry of unease ruffled low in her abdomen at the sight of his cock, huge and swollen, rising from a nest of golden fleece at his groin. It was thick, and reddened, and part of her was worried all over again about how it could ever fit into her without pain. Then again…she looked at his hand, with his long, thick fingers, recalling clearly how hard he'd made her come just moments ago, and the unease turned to excitement. Everything with Marc was so different—*so much better*. Why should this be an exception?

In spite of how obviously turned-on he was, Marc didn't so much as fidget, allowing her to look her fill without doing anything to intimidate her, and she loved him even more for it. He was no teddy bear. *Ah, non…* Teddy bears weren't trained killers. And yet, she'd always sensed that at his core, instead of brutality or even aggression, there was tenderness. She didn't think he would thank her for pointing it out, though, so she just smiled.

"Speechless?" he asked, obviously trying for a teasing tone but not entirely keeping a hint of vulnerability out of his voice.

"*Ah, oui,*" she agreed. "You're *splendide, mon amant.* I can't decide which part to touch first." She meant to tease, but she was serious. Her palms practically itched to touch him. Seized by a wild imp of mischief, and maybe by the need to confirm that, no matter what she did, he wouldn't betray her trust, she reached directly for his length, circling it with both hands.

His back nearly bowed off the bench, and the veins in his neck bulged as he made an inarticulate sound, but he didn't grab for her or force her underneath him. He just breathed quickly, harshly, as she slowly stroked up and down, marveling at the velvety hardness.

"Baby...*fuck*, you do not mess around, and your hands feel so good," he said in a strangled, breathless voice. "I know I said you could touch me anywhere...and you *can*...but I have to warn you that I'm so worked up from before, I don't think I'll be able to hold on for much more of that. I just...don't want to surprise you."

Tenderness and desire for Marc warred in her chest. She loved that he'd forego his own pleasure, again, to warn her. Then again, she wasn't sure that there was anything she didn't love about this man.

"We can't have that," she purred, releasing him so that he groaned. "Anywhere, you said?" She scooted up next to him to run her hands over his shoulders, arms, chest...everywhere she could reach. She kept her touch deliberately light, but she could see it was affecting Marc by the rapid rise and fall of his chest, by the way he bit his lip and his cock twitched. She reveled in the feeling of safety it gave her, of intimacy...that he would make himself so open to her. When she realized she was subconsciously trying to memorize every part of him, a lump formed in her throat, and she had to swallow, *hard*.

She wasn't sure how this was going to turn out. *God knows, someone has been one step ahead of us the whole time*, she thought, but when she looked back down at Marc's face, rough with the strain of holding himself back for her, a wave of emotion rushed over her, both warming and centering her. *Bon Dieu*, if she was only going to have a few stolen moments for her memories, she was going to make them count.

When she lowered to kiss his swollen sex, simultaneously circling the base with her hands, the sexy sound he made, like a combination between a grunt and a whimper, made her core go liquid all over again. She started with little open-mouthed kisses, then licked along his length. She worried he might accidentally thrust up and choke her if she took him fully into her mouth, but he held himself mostly still. When she dared a glance at his face, there was sweat beading on his forehead, and she knew that he wouldn't lose control.

In one fluid motion, she took as much of him as she could into the cavern of her mouth, and he groaned, low and sexy, balling his fists at his sides.

"Oh, God, baby…Clo…so fucking good. You feel fucking amazing…" He was breathing so hard, he could barely get the words out. "Dreamed of this so many times…not gonna last."

She continued to suck him and stroke him, more turned on than she could have imagined by his obvious pleasure.

"Baby, you should move now...or I'm gonna come in your mouth."

She kept working his cock with her lips and tongue, catching his eyes with hers and giving a little shake of her head. She wanted that...wanted all of him. He was *hers*.

He threw his head back with a hoarse shout and her mouth and throat filled with his hot release, slightly salty, which she swallowed, continuing to suck him until he stopped quivering. Only when he was limp beneath her did she release him with a slight pop, making him groan again. His panting was loud in the quiet room, and she crawled up his body, settling right next to him as he curled one arm heavily around her as if the motion was almost too much effort. They lay there like that for long moments, the slight sheen of sweat on his chest making their skin slide together. She didn't know if she'd ever felt happier.

"You liked it?" she asked, muffled against his chest.

His low chuckle was dark and sexy. "Baby, I loved it. That was, hands-down, the most intense experience I have ever had."

She lifted her head to look at him in surprise. "But...I thought you were probably experienced?" She made it a question. "You were *married*."

He shook his head slowly. "When I'm with you, Clo, nobody else matters."

She gave him a skeptical look and his answering smile was wry.

"I know it's cheesy, baby. Ridiculous, even. Doesn't mean it isn't true."

She wanted to believe him, but...how could she?

He sighed, making the parts of her body that were draped over him rise and fall with his movements, so that she felt as if they were interconnected.

"I can see that I have some more work to do, hmm-m?" he said playfully, rolling onto his side. She'd thought she couldn't possibly get turned on again for at least a few hours, but he proved her wrong, again, licking and stroking her until she agreed that she believed him and they drifted off together, curled under the stars and two blankets.

# Chapter Twelve

Marc woke up feeling curiously bereft, and only when he realized that the place next to him where Clothilde had lain was cold did he recognize the emotion. And shit, that wasn't good, because no matter how things went down, he probably had a long string of mornings waking up alone to look forward to. Close on the heels of that thought, though, was instant worry as to where she had gone. After what they'd shared the night before, he couldn't picture her sneaking off...although maybe he'd done something to spook her after all.

*You should have told her that you love her*, his inner romantic whispered. His inner romantic obviously didn't care that that kind of declaration could make things harder for her in the long run, he decided, quashing that impulse firmly. Without anything else to wear, he draped the blanket back over himself and padded down the stairs into the study by way of the tiny, attached bathroom.

The view that met him in the wood-paneled room was as surprising as it was welcome. Clothilde had obviously put her T-shirt back on and nothing else, which he could tell since she had bent over to open one of the lower doors of one of the massive, ornate combination bookcase-cabinets that lined the room. His cock leaped to attention at the way the fabric rode up just enough to expose the lower curves of her ass cheeks. It swelled even larger, almost painfully, when she crowed triumphantly and stood with a bounce, making her unbound breasts jiggle under the thin shirt. He was so distracted by how enticing she looked that he almost missed what she held.

"I knew it!" she said, setting down what appeared to be a somewhat dusty, leather-bound book, like a photo album, onto the desk closest to her.

He cleared his throat and felt something under his toe which he recognized were his boxer-briefs and slacks, still crumpled on the floor from the past night. He pulled them on rapidly, not wanting to scare her with his massive erection first thing in the morning, although he couldn't for the life of him remember where he might have thrown his shirt—or had she thrown it?

Semi-dressed, he came up behind her and moved her hair aside, kissing the back of her neck until she leaned back into him with gratifying speed. "Morning," he mumbled.

"Mm-m...good morning. That feels nice," she murmured, wiggling her ass against his groin so that he stifled a groan.

Looking over her shoulder, he saw that he'd been right, and it was a photo album open in front of her.

"What did you know, baby, that made you leave me and come down here alone?" he asked, trying not sound as peevish as he felt. Only...it wasn't the morning wake-up he'd expected.

She laughed, a silvery sound that rose over the ever-present noise from the rough surf through the still-open windows. "Ah, *mon pauvre petit chou*...did you have plans for me this morning, then?"

She surprised a laugh out of him, and he stepped closer into her body, running his hands briefly up and down her sides.

"I'm not a little anything," he teased, in reference to her calling him the equivalent of a poor little sweetie.

She leaned back against him, wiggling her hips again. "I can feel that," she answered, her voice slightly throaty, before she seemed to recollect herself and straightened, much to his regret. "But as I started to wake up, I remembered that the pictures of Raoul's mother—you remember, Élodie's new fiancé that you met at the gala?—they aren't in Montreal. Or at least, not all of them. I had totally forgotten that my mother used to keep some here, and they were just where I remembered!" She sounded triumphant as she turned in his arms, so that her breasts were practically pressed against his chest.

"That couldn't have waited until later?" he grumbled, kissing the side of her neck. She swatted at him playfully, but her breathing quickened.

"*Mais non*, because I knew that I would get distracted by your, you know, *manliness*—" She gestured with one hand.

"Is that what we're going to call it?" he prompted, raising one eyebrow, and she laughed again. Goddamn, she was unbelievably beautiful in the morning, even with the faint marks from the cushion still on her cheek...maybe *especially* with the marks on her cheek, since she'd been sleeping next to him. *I wish I could wake up like this every fucking day*, he thought.

"Yes, manliness seems...apropos, does it not?" She wiggled her eyebrows and caressed his hardness so briefly that he might have thought he'd imagined it except for the wicked sparkle in her chocolate-brown eyes. "But this is important...or, I think it might be. Something is just clanging about this... Something about Raoul's mother."

"Clanging?" he asked.

She pursed her lips, cocking her head. "Clanging, grating, bothering...you know."

He pushed all his playfulness away, the calculated special ops soldier returning. "Ah, of course. Let's take a look, then," he answered, motioning her toward the desk.

"It could be nothing," she warned, sitting in the desk chair as he pulled up another.

He knew it — *expected it* to be another dead end — but he couldn't help the flare of hope in his chest. After so long at a disadvantage, always one step behind, could something in this book give them the clue they needed?

The first few photos were pretty much what one would expect, a few shots of a much-younger version of a man Marc recognized as Clothilde's father, very dashing, on a sailboat. His smile was reminiscent of Rémy's in particular, charming, and whoever he was looking at — almost certainly his wife — obviously held his entire heart. Clothilde's expression was wistful.

"I never knew him like this...or, not for long enough for me to remember. He was never the same after

*Maman* got sick. I would have liked to have known this man, though, I think."

Marc put his hand over hers briefly, and she flashed him a small smile of gratitude. When she flipped to the next page, Marc sucked in a surprised breath. The woman beaming out, radiating happiness, from the photograph could have been Clothilde's sister...practically her twin.

"Holy—" He cut himself off, embarrassed, but Clothilde didn't seem perturbed.

"It's striking, *non*? Everyone always says how much I look like her."

She seemed a bit proud, and a bit...something else. Something Marc couldn't quite put his finger on.

"She is really...striking is right," he answered lamely. It truly looked like Clothilde, dressed in eighties clothing, hanging from the side of the same sailboat. "She glows...just like you. She must have been spectacular."

Clothilde stared at him, her eyes shiny. *"Mon amour...*what a lovely thing to say."

He felt his cheeks grow warm and knew that his pale complexion was probably betraying him with a dull flush on his skin. "It's...the truth," he answered gruffly, and she leaned over, planting an open-mouthed kiss on his surprised lips.

The sound of her flipping another page, this one sticking slightly, seemed loud, but that could have been his discomfort talking. She finally got the two pages separated, with some gentle coaxing. At first, the pictures seemed almost to be from another album entirely, groups of men in uniform.

Two of them seemed vaguely familiar though. "Wait! Is that—?"

Clothilde sucked in a sharp breath. "That's Jean-Marie de Voltin, Claude's father, with Armand Carillon."

Marc studied the photo, trying to make sense of what he was seeing. To his knowledge — which should have been extremely thorough indeed after nearly two years on this op — none of the potential players should have been military, but here were Jean-Marie de Voltin and Armand Carillon in what appeared to be Canadian Air Force uniforms. There was nothing special about the pose, just young men grinning at the camera in front of a plane, looking as if they felt invincible. *Shit*, Marc had *been* in his own version of this type of photo with Cob. Cob's grandma had kept hers in a frame in the living room for years. But how had he not known that de Voltin was former Canadian military?

Also... "Who's the third man? Do you recognize him? Or anyone else in the background?" Marc thought the features of the man standing between Carillon and de Voltin looked vaguely familiar, but he couldn't place him.

Clothilde nodded thoughtfully. "I feel like I may have met one of the men in the background, though I can't say for certain. For the man with his arms around Armand and Jean-Marie, I'm not positive, but...I think that might be Georges de Sancy."

"Raoul's father?" Marc looked at the young man's features again, and he couldn't see much similarity, but he could just make out the name tag that the young man wore. "Holy shit, I think you're right." He looked at the plane behind them. It wasn't a run-of-the mill plane, though. It was ultra-high-tech, especially for the 1980s, when the photo had obviously been taken.

"What the *hell* are they doing in uniform, with a fighter jet like that?"

Clothilde looked as puzzled as he felt. "I really don't know. Even Pierre probably doesn't, since these pictures look like they're from before or maybe right after he was born."

She flipped through a couple of more pages, which seemed more typical, joyful young men and women at parties, a few holding babies or opening presents.

When she got to a page that had a picture of a young couple, obviously deeply enamored, she pointed to it with a cry. "Oh, here's the picture I was thinking of... I *knew* we had pictures of Eveline de Sancy, Raoul's mother."

Marc studied the photo. Raoul must take after his mother because, where Marc had not really recognized traits in common between Raoul and his father, the woman in the picture could have been the younger man's sister. Her face was striking, and in the picture, it was practically luminous with the clear adoration she turned on her companion. He was obviously young, with dark hair, but he was mostly turned away from the camera so it was impossible to recognize him with certainty. Still, he was extremely tall...unlike the man who would become her husband. "She was lovely...but that doesn't appear to be Georges de Sancy."

Clothilde's expression grew distant, troubled. "Oh, *non*...but I think I know who it is. I just remembered something...something I believe I haven't thought of for a long time. *Bon Dieu*, I think...maybe Claude begged me to forget so much that I really tried to, but looking at this, I remember everything."

She looked so stricken that Marc wanted nothing more than to pull her into his arms and run, away from this—whatever it was—and the rest of their problems. He wished he didn't know better, that realistically, they could never really escape. Whatever she'd remembered could be the key to keeping her safe.

"Baby, whatever Claude said or did to you—and I know he did plenty—he can't hurt you anymore. *We* made sure of that. You are so strong, so brave…and I'm here to help you face whatever you remember."

He held her gaze, willing her to feel his strength and determination, to use it as her own. She tilted up her chin, her expression becoming resolved…resilient. Not for the first time, he marveled at her strength, so well-hidden and guarded from almost everyone else.

Clothilde took a deep breath before she continued. "When I was *très petite*, Papa and Jean-Marie—you know, Claude's father?—took just Claude and me out sailing. Luc was supposed to come, too, but he had…oh, what's the English word. *Varicelle*?"

"Chicken pox?" Marc offered, and she smiled weakly.

"Oh, yes, that's it…such a funny name. But *oui*, Luc had the chicken pox, and he was crushed to have to stay home. It was a rare day, after *Maman* got sick, when our father was in a good mood. She must have been feeling better—she would have these temporary reprieves sometimes—and he'd felt comfortable leaving her alone for a while. I couldn't have been more than five or six, and it started off as a glorious day." She looked wistful. "I didn't know there would be so few," she said quietly. "But everything we talked about is sort of stamped in my memory, in spite of my trying to pretend the rest of the day didn't happen."

Marc squeezed her shoulder. "Makes sense," he said, hating the pain on her face and in her voice.

"I think you know this, but Jean-Marie de Voltin really was like an uncle to all of us, and he was Papa's closest friend. Our families spent a ton of time together. It was part of why it was so natural for me to get together with Claude when he started pursuing me. Like my father, Jean-Marie was charming, funny, smart. He was just wonderful, in my childish mind, anyway. He died when I was still young, not long after Papa, so I only have those impressions of him. We stopped on an island for a picnic lunch, and Claude and I ran into the woods to get sticks for kindling." She paused and looked at him. "I haven't let myself think about this in years, and it might not be important at all…just a young girl's memories."

Marc ran the back of one hand down her cheek. "First, *everything* you say is important to me, Clo," he said, coming dangerously close to revealing his feelings. He really didn't want to do that…not when he was likely going to be unable to be a part of her life, and it would be selfish to burden her with them or ask her to wait. He cleared his throat uncomfortably. "Second, anything could be significant, even the smallest detail."

Her smile was small. "*Bon, alors*…we were gathering wood, and we must have returned more quietly than they expected, because they were still talking in hushed voices when we got back. Jean-Marie said something like, '*I never should have married her, Guillaume. She was just so devastated when Georges married Eveline out of the blue. But she can barely stand me or the boy…treats us as if we weren't even there. I think she feels like we trap her — like maybe she could leave if we hadn't had a baby.*' And I remember Claude's face was so stricken. Even though we'd known his mother was kind of, well, *cold*, it was harsh to hear his father say that."

"I can imagine," Marc answered, feeling an unwilling stirring of sympathy for the boy Claude had been. He had no sympathy for the man...but to hear *that* as a young child? *Wow.* "Did you hear them say anything else?" Marc's senses were on high alert. Something told him this might well be the heart of the motivation for someone.

Clothilde nodded. "Yes. I'm pretty sure I remember almost exactly how my father answered, because he used bad language that seemed pretty scandalous to me at the time. He said something like, '*You thought you were doing the right thing. How could you have known? I hold myself to blame. If I hadn't gotten us roped into that shitstorm of a project, Armand would never have gone missing...and Eveline would never have thought he'd abandoned her. Even now, your Caroline could be happily married to Georges, and Armand to Eveline.*'"

"Wait, *shit!* So it's *Armand Carillon* who's in the picture with Eveline de Sancy?" Marc didn't really need Clothilde's nod of confirmation, as his mind racing ahead to put the pieces together. "Okay, that info, combined with the other picture in uniforms, and it sounds like your father was probably talking about a military project, which he must have been involved with, too. Makes sense, since he probably wouldn't have this type of photo with advanced tech otherwise. If he caused one of his friends to go missing and their girls married men who they didn't love, including Claude's parents...that's a *hell* of a lot of motivation, sweetheart." His heart felt a pang of sympathy as he looked down at the woman's expression, captured forever on film in this dusty old album. For a woman who felt that way about him, a man might do just about anything.

Guarded by a Hero

When Marc looked over at her, Clothilde looked upset. No, she looked more than upset— She looked racked with guilt. "I wish I'd thought of this sooner…realized the connection. It's just that, at the time, Claude was devastated. Like, it almost made him seem a bit scary. He made me swear I would forget it, never speak of it. I was so young, and he frightened me, but I still loved him so I… Well, I think I just blocked it out. I would probably still be blocking it out if we hadn't come looking for the photos."

Grabbing her hand and squeezing, Marc considered their conversation with Armand, Élodie and Raoul at the gala two days earlier. Everything now took on a sinister tilt, Armand's surprise appearance, but also Raoul de Sancy.

"Baby, it's not your fault. You were a child, and even if you *did* remember that Claude's parents didn't love each other—not uncommon, unfortunately—that doesn't mean that there would have a been a connection to some sort of criminal mastermind. I'm just glad we remembered…but suspicious of what prompted you to come looking."

Clothilde was likely trying to furrow her brow, but she only managed to look beautiful and consternated. "Raoul? *Non.* I mean, I don't really know him, but Élodie has been my friend my whole life, and I think she would know if he were a criminal."

"Baby, Claude was your friend, too," he reminded gently.

Clothilde's head snapped to look at him directly, her eyes stormy. "You do not mince your words much, do you, Mr. Constantin?"

He hated that he might have hurt her, but he wasn't sorry that he'd gotten her attention. "I'm a plain-spoken man, for better or worse. But you have to be suspicious of everyone at this point, Clo. It's too dangerous not to be. We need to find out more about Armand Carillon and Raoul de Sancy." He chose not to mention that he was going to have to investigate Élodie Carillon, too.

"What about you?" she shot back, with spirit. "If I'm not supposed to trust my friends, family friends — nobody — how do you know you can trust your whole unit?"

*Stupid, stupid, stupid.* Clothilde's words hit their mark, and he realized that the answer to why progress had been so damned slow throughout the op might have been staring him plain in the face. "Fuck it all…you're absolutely right."

Marc stood abruptly, his mind racing. If these key players — Carillon, de Voltin, de Sancy and Guillaume Gaspard himself — had been military or had military connections, it meant someone had been lying to them from the get-go…keeping critical details from his entire team. It changed *everything*. "I'm gonna call in some favors for confidential intel. Clark, Barnes and Castellano can help me, but I'm not trusting anyone else."

Clothilde nodded, her previous anger obviously replaced by concern. "Okay."

He bent to kiss her almost absently, his mind already half-occupied with who to call and what, specifically, to ask them for. "Good work, Duchess. Real good work."

# Chapter Thirteen

"These have to be the best pancakes…er, what did you call these things?" Brian rubbed his stomach in appreciation, sitting at the thick kitchen table, which was made from reclaimed boat wood.

"*Des crêpes*," she answered, grinning when he grimaced at her French pronunciation, which sounded like *crehp*, with a guttural R.

"Ma'am…I just, I can't call these 'crap', no matter if that *is* the correct word in French," Brian answered.

Castellano, who she'd just learned bore the incongruous first name of Finnian, interjected. "We Americans usually just mispronounce them as '*craypes*'." He turned a winning smile toward Clothilde. "Not meaning to spoil your fun, ma'am."

"Oh, no fair!" she teased, waving her spatula in the air. "No Nutella for you on the next one!"

The junior soldier took her ribbing good-naturedly. "I was about to switch with Barnes anyway, to give him a chance to sample some of your delicious cooking as well, so I think that's my cue," he answered, and pushed open the thick door—original to the lighthouse—to let in a cool gust of sea air.

Marc and Barnes were already on their way in, though. Clothilde's heart sank right down into her gut at the grim expressions on their faces.

"No need to come out. I want us to have a team meeting…the five of us." Marc looked at each person in turn, including her, as if giving them a good chance to object, but nobody spoke and the door banged closed.

Clothilde crossed the room to embrace him, uncaring now if the other men saw them. Marc wore a sweater with a thicker cable knit against the cold wind gusts, which had grown a bit chilly for the summer, and his chest felt cool and damp against her cheek, smelling a bit like a salty fisherman. He wrapped his arms around her for an instant before stepping back to address the room.

"You didn't learn anything good, did you?" she guessed, but now that she could generally read his stoic expressions, she could tell that whatever he had to say, they weren't going to like it.

"Nope…I did not. What I'm about to say doesn't leave this room, but I think we're going to have to cross the line here, so if anyone doesn't want to be a part of it, I won't judge you for leaving here now." Again, he waited, but there wasn't a breath of movement from any of the other four people there.

Marc gave the ghost of a smile. "All right, then. One of my old unit has a buddy who was willing to go deep to get the info—hopefully without leaving a trace, and if I would trust anyone to do that, it's this kid—and the probable head of the criminal activity, who we call the Chimère, is not only incredibly wealthy and powerful, but he's one of our own." Lines of strain bracketed his mouth. "Worse, they knew it and played us — played *me* — from the start. Someone high up has suspected all along who it might be."

Clothilde sat down heavily on the weather-beaten wooden kitchen chair. "That means...all this time, they could have protected us...my family."

Marc blew out a pained breath. "I'm so sorry, sweetheart." He'd had the same realization himself, along with the fact that someone could have spoken out sooner and saved Cob as well, along with countless others.

"Menzies?" Clark asked, and Clothilde dragged her gaze away from the table to look at him. He looked almost impassive — they all did — but his eyes gave him away. They were thunderous.

"Who or what is Menzies?" she asked.

"My old friend from the courtroom," Marc replied. "Aside from the men in this room, he's been the closest to the op...and he's the one who gives us our intel and orders." He turned to address Clark. "And I don't know whether he was in on this or not. He's always hinted at pressure from higher up, but that could have been to cover himself. On the other hand, if we don't follow up with him, to be sure, we leave him flapping in the wind."

The three younger soldiers looked troubled.

Barnes spoke first. "I say we try to feel him out during your next call. When is it?"

If possible, Marc's expression darkened. "That's the thing. He called me twice, off-schedule, and missed our last check-in time."

"*Fuck*, that's not good — uh, sorry, ma'am." Clark looked contrite.

Clothilde waved away the apology. "Oh, *non*, I'm with you, *bordel*."

"It sounds so much prettier when you swear, though, baby," Marc commented, and the tension felt like it had been cut in half.

"*Merci*, asshole," she answered with a cheeky grin, surprising chuckles out of all the men.

"I stand by my comment," Marc returned, bending down to whisper in her ear. "And you can call me anything you want with that pretty mouth of yours."

She flushed hot at his rumbling tone and flashed him a warning glare. They weren't alone, after all.

Marc straightened, becoming all business again. "For Menzies, the way I see it, there are two possibilities. First, he's been in on it and has now hung us out to dry. He's one of the very few people who know exactly where we are, what defenses we have and could seriously screw us over. We're basically sitting ducks here if he has flipped."

All amusement had faded from the other men's faces as he spoke.

"Second," he continued, "Menzies is just as much of a pawn as we are, in which case his silence could mean a lot of things...but nothing good."

Barnes, who was generally the quietest of the three, cleared his throat. "I can't speak for anyone else, but even though he's a real tight-ass SOB, I respect him. I have a hard time seeing Menzies being in on this."

Castellano nodded. "He's the one who brought me on board. I don't always like him, but he's a hell of a loyal soldier."

"Never leave a brother behind...if we're voting," Clark said, looking to Marc. Marc was still in charge, she realized.

"Noted…and agreed," Marc answered grimly.

The door blew open with a loud crack against the wall, and a dark figure appeared. *A huge man in a wetsuit?* she wondered but couldn't see because the men all leaped toward her — protecting her.

"I fucking hope so, since I swam a couple miles to save your sorry asses." The angry stranger's voice rang out in the stone-walled room.

"Menzies! How the hell — ?" Marc's voice was furious, cut off by the man.

"Did I get past your underwater sensors? They were disabled already, Constantin, and I'm guessing the buoys are, too, but I wasn't gonna surface and give anyone watching a target to shoot at, although I did reactivate the underwater ones." The stranger — Menzies — sounded more disgruntled than worried.

The door banged closed, and the four men closed more tightly around her. In fact, her face was essentially in Marc's ass, her nose a mere millimeter from it, and she had to stifle the completely absurd impulse to bite it. *Marc has obviously turned me into a sex maniac*, she thought wildly.

"If I'd wanted to kill Target Alpha, or any of you, I've had plenty of chances already, you know," Menzies continued. "You're practically stifling the young lady."

"We're not moving until you prove that you weren't in on the cover-up of intel, on the military backgrounds of de Voltin, Carillon, de Sancy and Gaspard…one of whom is almost certainly the Chimère." Marc's voice held a warning note.

Menzies' sigh was put-upon. "My balls are turning to ice after nearly too long in that fucking frigid water — and you know I'm Scottish, so I'm used to some pretty fecking glacial lochs—so I'm gonna make this quick. Are your weapons in easy reach?"

"Always, sir," Marc answered, and the other men chorused similar answers.

"Then three of you grab them and aim them at me, and for the love of Christ, the fourth man please go get me a towel and a blanket, since I'm apparently too goddamn old for field work."

Clothilde had to stifle a completely inappropriate giggle at how peeved Menzies sounded. Marc inclined his head in a small nod, which she could only see from the back of his head, but it seemed to be enough for the other men as they rapidly grabbed the weapons they'd apparently had stashed all over her kitchen. They were careful to keep two bodies in front of her at all times, almost as if they'd choreographed the moves—just like when Marc and Barnes had come to the rescue of her and Marina, she realized. When they were all armed, Castellano hurried into the next room, returning with the requested blanket and two towels in record time.

"If anyone has delicate sensibilities, turn away, lasses, because I'm serious about needing to check my balls for fucking frostbite. Just because my wife didn't particularly care for them anymore doesn't mean some other woman might not enjoy them someday."

This time, Clothilde couldn't quite stifle her snort of amusement.

"Clo," Marc said warningly, "he could be trying to put us at ease."

She heard something heavy and wet fall to the floor—almost certainly the wetsuit—then the rustling of fabric.

"Feeling well enough to talk now, sir?" Marc asked dryly.

"I'll live, Constantin…for now, at least. Our chances as a group aren't great, though, unless we can get to trusting each other again pretty fucking fast."

Clothilde tensed, and Marc must have felt it, because he put a reassuring hand behind him to touch her arm.

"I can see you listened to my order not to get too close to Target Alpha, too," Menzies added, his tone dripping with sarcasm.

"If I'd disobeyed sooner, maybe we could have solved this a lot more quickly, as well," Marc retorted.

"Yeah," Menzies answered, sounded defeated. "I figured that out during the time I had to think during my leisurely swim here."

When he answered, Marc sounded mollified. "All right, putting the past behind us since we all got played, what made you come here?"

Menzies sighed, and it sounded somehow guilty. "There is one thing that I did know that I was asked to keep from you — from all of you. It's about Pierre Gaspard."

Clothilde felt protective fury rise into her chest. "My brother is not the…whatever you called the mastermind, the Chimère, or in any way involved! He would never put Marina and I in danger that way — or himself, or our brothers — not anyone!"

"Slow your roll, Boadicea, and let me finish," Menzies answered, and she forced herself to calm and listen.

"Fine," she ground out.

"You're much feistier than your reputation would suggest," Menzies commented, but he didn't sound upset. On the contrary, in fact. "I can see why my men have all become so enamored by you."

"Why don't you finish what you were saying about Pierre," Marc growled.

"Pierre Gaspard has been a strong ally of the Canadian and US militaries," Menzies started.

"Right, I'm already aware of that," Marc replied, a little sharply. "He did some defense-only work, very clearly specified, which is why he has ongoing clearance."

"What you may not be aware of is that he has been doing ongoing work, and Luc has been as well, since he has been taking over more of the reins of the company over the past several months."

The room was so silent that Clothilde could hear the shutters banging on the outside of the house, in spite of the thick kitchen walls.

"This is all very highly classified, and the relationship continues to be defense-only. As you know, Gaspard Industries has some of the best tech in the world. It could potentially be used for many purposes, but Pierre, and now Luc, have always been adamant that they want to help humanity, so nothing is allowed to be developed, based on their designs, in an offensive capacity, and the tech remains proprietary to Gaspard Industries."

Clothilde's heart was thumping. She hadn't known, although she'd heard indirect rumors and whispers from other company insiders that Pierre had stopped a board takeover that would have made the company much more weapons-focused and possibly much more lucrative.

"That's interesting, but what does that have to do with why you decided to miss our check-in and swim to Wilson's Rock?" Marc prompted.

"I've been growing suspicious of the pressure from higher up for a while, as some of it seemed to conflict with some of our main objectives, so I was doing some digging and came across contracts dated from over a year ago authorizing offensive use of Gaspard Industries technology, reportedly signed by Pierre Gaspard." Clothilde gasped when Menzies paused. "The countersignature was redacted, though... redacted from my access, anyway, which is pretty fucking extensive."

Clothilde pushed at Marc's lower back. "Let me look around you. I want to see his face," she said.

"No, baby, you'll be exposed," Marc answered. She appreciated his caution, but *come on*.

"Didn't all of you just get a thorough look to check for concealed weapons?" she prompted dryly.

"Well, uh, yes...but he's dangerous without a weapon, too," Marc replied, but she could tell he was wavering.

"And you four are pussycats, *hein*?" she countered.

With a grumble, Marc moved slightly to one side, barely enough for her to look through the open space. Menzies was an imposing figure indeed, with his angry, red scar bisecting his face. He looked sincere, though.

"Who countersigned the other contracts with my brother?" she asked.

Menzies' blue eyes practically crackled with a combination of tension and anticipation. "Access denied. That's when it clicked, and I tried to call—which you didn't answer, so thanks for that—and headed out."

Clothilde mentally put the pieces together, and she could practically hear the others working it out as well.

"I vote to trust Menzies," she said, "and I think we need to call my brothers."

There were grunts of agreement from the other men.

"We'll still proceed with caution," Marc warned, his comment obviously directed mostly at Menzies.

"Thank fuck, because my feet are nearly as cold on this damned stone floor as my balls were in the ocean," Menzies answered, earning a glare from Marc. She hid another smile, but sobered immediately at Menzies' next words.

"Someone is coming…probably soon. Our only advantage is that they aren't aware that we're onto them. If they're watching—and I think they are—and we try to leave, we'll spoil that, so I think we're gonna have to make our stand here, now. Anything we can learn from your family might help us."

# Chapter Fourteen

"Clochette? Can you hear us?"

The feeling of relief that swept over her at the reassuring, gruff sound of her oldest brother, Pierre's, voice made her eyes suddenly sting with tears.

"*Oui,*" she croaked "I'm here, Pierrot."

"This thing...*putain de merde*...I can barely hear you! Villiers set this secured call up but we made him leave." Pierre's frustration was characteristic. As someone who had always had to be in charge of everything, he had a very low tolerance for technical difficulties. She heard a woman's voice murmuring soothingly in the background.

"*Salut*, Marina!" she called to her brother's girlfriend — really, the love of his life. She expected an official engagement any day.

"Hi, Clo! It's good to hear your voice. We've been so worried. I had to threaten to tie your brother up to keep him from coming to, um, where you are immediately."

Clothilde smiled at Marina's near-mistake. They were pretty confident that the line should be protected from everyone, but to be extra safe, they weren't planning on mentioning specific locations.

"As if you could tie me up," Pierre huffed, and Clothilde had to cough to cover a giggle when she heard a low feminine whisper that sounded like, '*You know you love it when I let you do it to me, so you owe me at least one.*'

"Might I remind you that there *are* other people on this call?" Luc sounded peeved, and tired. "*Single* people?"

"*Lu-louche*…is it too late for you? You didn't have to talk now." It was relatively late in Maine, so Clothilde realized it must be around two a.m. in France.

"I always have time for my brothers or sister, Clo. Sorry to be grumpy. I'm so happy to hear you sounding safe and well."

Luc's answer sounded almost like he was talking through a tin can, but she could still hear how genuine the words were, and they touched her. Her brothers had always rallied around her whenever she needed them.

"Is Rémy on, too?" Pierre demanded.

"I'm here…and so is Annelise, assuming that's okay?"

Clothilde smiled. Rémy had probably always been the most thoughtful and sensitive of her brothers.

"*More* than okay…Annelise and Marina are both family," Clothilde confirmed, realizing as she spoke the words that she truly meant them. She already loved Annelise and Marina like the sisters she'd never had.

"Oh, Clo…I feel the same way," Annelise answered, and Clothilde could practically feel a hug from both of them coming through the speakerphone in the small, extra-secured room where she sat.

Marc put his hands on her shoulders and rubbed, just once, but it was enough to remind her that she wasn't alone. He had proven, time and again, that he would be there for her.

"*Bon*, since everyone is here, before we say anything else, I just—" Clothilde's voice faltered and cracked, only for an instant.

"We can do this another way, baby," Marc murmured.

"Is that fucking Constantin with you? Because I have a lot to say to him," Pierre blasted. She didn't need to see his face to feel how furious he was.

She shook her head at Marc and cleared her throat. "Marc is here, and that's exactly how I want it. He has protected me and saved me, more times than you realize...but also, I care for him, deeply." She looked back at Marc. "I love him."

Her words fell heavily in the silent room, so muffled by the sound dampeners. Marc's face was unreadable, and Clothilde felt her heartbeat stutter. She didn't want to call the words back, though. They were true, and she wanted Marc to know.

"All right, Clochette. Of course," Pierre answered. They might disagree, but the Gaspards were always there for each other...*always*.

"You know you have our respect, Constantin," Rémy added.

"And I trust my sister, too," Luc confirmed.

"Fine, then. I'll continue. I wanted to tell you that I love you, and the way the three of you, *mes frères*, helped me put myself back together, not once but twice, in terrible circumstances... I thank you, from the bottom of my soul."

"Clo, I don't like that this sounds like you're going to do something dangerous," Pierre cautioned in his permanently gravelly voice.

"If there's danger, I want to be there, at least." Luc sounded like he was trying to lighten the mood, but there was a core of steel in his tone.

"*Mon Luc préféré*," she teased, and hated the little wobble in her voice. She'd always called him that when they were young — her favorite Luc — since she couldn't call him her favorite brother with two other brothers she loved so much.

"Now you're really scaring me, Clochette," he answered.

"Me, too," Pierre agreed.

"You know we can't handle it when you're nice to us," Rémy added.

"I don't think any of you would be able to make it here quickly enough to help in-person —" she started.

"Rémy and I are the closest. We'll both leave right now, *ma puce*... You just sit tight," Pierre interrupted, and the fierce love and determination she heard in his voice made her heart squeeze in her chest. She looked up at Marc and saw tenderness in his expression. He gave a little shrug, and she understood. He didn't think they would make it, but he was happy to have them if she wanted.

"I appreciate that, but I want you safe — *all* of you." She meant it. No matter what, she wanted Pierre and Rémy, who had so recently found love and peace, to have long, wonderful lives, with lots of little nieces and nephews, whether she got to meet them or not.

"I'm already on my way," Luc interjected. "And before you ask him, no, Constantin didn't call me. I got a bad feeling about something I overheard at a meeting. I figured I was overreacting, but now..." He let his words trail off.

"Was it a meeting with a military contact?" Marc asked.

The silence over the line was heavy, as if everyone was gauging everyone else. They had decided with Menzies in advance that her family could be temporarily authorized to know everything, so Clothilde decided to take charge.

"I'm going to speed this up. *Bref*, Marc is actually not a security guard, but he's still in special unit of the military, along with Clark, Barnes and Castellano — oh, Castellano's new, but really nice. Pierre apparently already knew that Marc was active-duty special ops, and Luc probably knew, too, although that I'm not sure of. P.S., I'm super pissed at both of you — because they have military clearance and defense-only military contracts for Gaspard Industries tech. I figure we can work out all our righteous anger later, assuming none of us are dead. Are we all on the same page?"

There was a short pause.

"Bravo, girl!" came Marina's voice first. "And solidarity. Pierre and I are going to have a discussion later, but I know I can say that we always have your back."

"Um, Rémy's looking...less-than-calm, with that vein in his neck popping out — you know the one — so I'm gonna just chime in for us and say that we appreciate the info and we're behind you one hundred percent." Annelise's diplomatic response made Clothilde both amused and deeply concerned. She did know the vein...and while Rémy was generally slow to anger, when he got good and steamed, everyone needed to watch out.

"Luc, why don't you answer Constantin — and I'm interested in your answer, too — then we can see what else they need?" Pierre's voice was firm and steady, and Clothilde was reminded of why he was the undisputed head of the Gaspard family, even if he was no longer the official head of their company. He'd always been there for his siblings, and she'd only recently learned what toll it had taken on him.

"*Bon*, it was indeed a military meeting, and I'm on a military plane. Did I mention that I recently got certified as a jet pilot? Don't worry — I bought this one. Cost a pretty penny, too. Solange in Accounting just about laid an egg." His voice sounded like it was a fond memory.

Clothilde remembered Solange. She would have enjoyed antagonizing her, too. She was an old busybody — but very good at her job.

"What spooked you at the meeting?" Marc prompted.

"Sorry...pretty tired," Luc apologized. "I saw someone I hadn't seen in a long time. Thought I was seeing a ghost."

"Luc, I believe they're on a pretty tight schedule right now," Pierre said laconically.

"It looked for all the world like Michel Montfort," Luc continued. "I briefly questioned my sanity, then drove off base like a bat out of hell, which luckily for me is my typical speed or someone might have been concerned."

"Michel Montfort? But he died in the plane crash with Jean-Marie de Voltin. There were no survivors."

Rémy's voice was grave. They had all been devastated by the loss of Jean-Marie, especially since it hadn't been that long after their father's death.

"Michel Montfort was friends with our father and Jean-Marie, and the rumor was that he was a significant financial backer of Jean-Marie de Voltin's Middle Eastern venture," Pierre explained, obviously for Marc's benefit. Clothilde tried to picture Montfort's face, but she only remembered heavy cigarette smoke and bad breath.

"I know it was reported that he had died...and of course, it was odd, because he wore a French-Canadian military uniform. It was a joint meeting, involving collaboration. He looked older, but I knew immediately who he was," Luc answered. "You remember his nose, don't you, Clochette? Pretty distinctive."

"*Oh mon Dieu, oui!*" Clothilde exclaimed, forgetting to speak in English. "He came to the house a few times with Jean-Marie and Armand after *Maman* died, when Pierre and Rémy were away at school. He was awful... I never liked him. I thought of him as oily—like he would be kind and soft with Papa but then mean with the staff. I saw him kick our cook's little dog once, but he lied and said the dog fell off the terrace ledge. The poor thing had two broken ribs."

"You're certain it was him, Luc?" Marc prompted.

"As sure as I can be without DNA, yes," Luc confirmed. "He was walking with my primary contact, Colonel Lafond."

Now that she'd remembered the odious man, his face was fresh in her memory, and she thought she'd seen him somewhere else recently, too.

"Marc," she said urgently, turning around in her chair to take his arm. "I just realized who the man was in the background of the military photo in the album...the one who looked familiar. It was Michel Montfort."

"Well, shit, sweetheart. I think we can guess who the higher-up officer was who was putting pressure on Menzies," Marc answered, his mouth set in a grim line.

"I think Annelise and I might have seen something interesting, too." Rémy sounded pensive.

"Anything could help. We've just been chasing shadows lately — or that's what it's felt like," Marc admitted.

"You know we've been doing a real social whirl lately, what with our engagement and everyone else being otherwise occupied." Rémy was obviously trying to be nice, but Clothilde knew that with Luc in Europe, her in Boston and Pierre at Marina's side as she recovered quietly on their estate in Montreal, Rémy and Annelise had basically been forced to represent the Gaspards at any recent important events.

"We so appreciate that. I hope you know that we do, especially since it's really not your favorite thing," she said, with feeling.

Rémy chuckled. "It's not, but I'll admit, any excuse to see my Annelise in a gown — or take her out of one — is fine by me."

"Rémy!" Annelise squeaked, and his siblings groaned.

"Too much information!" Clothilde cried. "Make it stop!" She looked up at Marc to share her amusement — *and how freaking corny could Rémy get?*

Marc smiled, but his eyes were like steel, focused, and she immediately sobered.

"What was it that you saw?" Marc prompted.

"It was about two weeks ago. We actually met Colonel Lafond." It was Annelise who answered. "We went to that benefit for the wonderful veteran's center in Boston. It was relatively typical, although very well done—ballroom, live band, dinner—except of course there were a lot of men and women in uniform, current and former servicemembers. The speaker was superb. I cried twice."

"*Chérie*," Rémy said, in a voice so achingly tender it made Clothilde's insides feel mushy.

"Right, Colonel Lafond. I remember him because he was standing with the speaker, who I had really wanted to meet. He excused himself almost as soon as I joined their conversation, though. He said he saw someone he had to speak with and went over to your friends from the aquarium gala."

Clothilde could have sworn she felt electricity prickle on her skin, and her arm hairs stood up. "Which friends?" she asked.

"The older gentleman, Armand Carillon, and his daughter…that gorgeous blonde Élodie."

"Élodie was there?" she asked, feeling sick. Élodie had distinctly implied that she'd been with her mother, unable to get away at all for weeks until the night of the gala.

"She was definitely there. I remember because you had introduced me to her specifically, since she's your good friend from school. Plus, she's pretty striking with that natural blonde hair. I tried to find her to say hi, but she disappeared." Annelise's observation made it impossible to ignore that Élodie Carillon might be somehow involved, something that Clothilde really hadn't even wanted to consider.

"What about Raoul de Sancy?" Marc followed up.

"Oh, the French-Canadian Cary Grant?" Annelise started.

Clothilde couldn't help an unwilling smile at her future sister-in-law's description, which was pretty much spot-on.

"Definitely not. I would have remembered seeing him for sure, but I never met him before the gala," Annelise affirmed.

"That's extremely helpful. Thank you," Marc answered, with feeling. "And now I think we have to share all this with our team. Luc, do you have a way to keep us posted?"

"I can't tell you much, other than that I'll likely be dropping and swimming, but I can stealth past anything that can't physically see me."

Clothilde was suddenly very, very worried about what had been going with her youngest brother lately, but it wasn't the time to ask. Still, she made a mental note to talk to him, *soon*, provided she made it through the night.

"How do you — ?" Marc shook his head. "You know what? I don't think I should ask, so I'll just give the other guys a heads-up."

"*Please* be careful, Luc," she said, meaning the words deeply.

"I know you have to go, but I just want to say one more thing, Clochette." Rémy's voice cracked on her name, and Clothilde's vision grew a little blurry. "I know that Pierre and Luc feel the same, because we've talked about it. You are the *trésor* of the Gaspards — our treasure — and we couldn't have asked for a better sister. I hope I get to deliver another version of this speech at your wedding, and at the christening of your firstborn, and every family event thereafter. Marc, we're trusting you."

Marc put his hands on her shoulders. "I'll protect her until the last breath leaves my body," he vowed, and she felt the weight of his words like a blanket, settling over and around her.

Turning her head so she could look up at him again, she answered, "Then I'll do the same, Marc."

There was a moment of silence then a chorus of '*I love yous*' from her family before they hung up the secured call.

# Chapter Fifteen

Everything Marc's small team—and Menzies had really been invaluable—had been able to discover on Michel Montfort and Armand Carillon pointed to one or both of them being the Chimère. Whatever they were, they were both liars into the business of deception up to their eyeballs. The big question marks were Élodie and Raoul.

Marc was kicking himself for not seeing it sooner. Because Armand Carillon had been a last-minute guest at the gala at the aquarium, they'd done an abbreviated background check on him, his daughter and her fiancé and turned up nothing on the surface. However, now that they'd dug deeper, while the evidence of his past history with the military must be buried under layers of protections, they could see suspicious gaps in the personal histories of all of them.

If he'd been alone, or alone with just his team, on Wilson's Rock, he would have been waiting with the usual mix of excitement and fear that he fucking lived for. He longed to catch the Chimère, to avenge Cob and the Gaspards, but most of all, he longed for all this to be over. He was sick of the intrigue and deception, questioning everything and everyone. With Clothilde here, though, he felt none of his usual excitement — absolutely no thrill of battle to come. *Hell no.* Looking at the lovely, kind, caring, brilliant woman he'd come to love deeply and with whom he feared no amount of time would ever be enough, he felt naked terror.

"Baby, I wish you would go into the safe room," he urged again, just as he had been for the past thirty minutes since they'd met with their small team. "Someone is coming for you, to silence what you know. We're all highly trained professionals."

"And I have already proven to you that I am an excellent markswoman — or did you forget that I hit a superior range of targets in the simulations you insisted I demonstrate to you before you would let me carry my own weapon back in Boston?" she countered.

"I know…and damn, Duchess, you don't know how sexy I thought you were when you nailed all those shots, then gave me that triumphant little smirk." He smiled a little at the recollection. "But the reality is that the rest of us have combat experience, keeping cool under attack, which no amount of training can totally prepare you for." He tried to speak gently, but he wasn't sure he'd succeeded since she looked mutinous. "What's more, I just can't handle the thought of you being in danger. It rips me up inside, thinking you could be hurt or killed. Even though we know that they likely won't bring a big strike force, whoever they bring is gonna be professional. They won't have surprise on their side, but they'll still have weapons. We can't even assume that they're rogue agents, except for the

Chimère himself. They could be operatives following orders, and I don't want to take out anyone except the major players...and we want to take them in alive as well, if at all possible. It's gonna be really damn tricky, especially with just five of us, no matter how elite others might consider us."

She stepped closer to him, looking troubled. *How wrong is it that I find her even more breathtaking in black leggings and a black sweater with a ponytail than I did in her pretty evening gowns?* he wondered.

"Let's all go in the safe room, then," she implored.

He shook his head. "First, your brother is coming, and we're not letting him walk into a shitstorm alone." He stepped closer until they were practically chest-to-chest, taking her face into his hands. Her skin was petal-soft against his fingertips. "Second, if we don't bring in the Chimère, we're just rogue operators. At best, we'll be locked up for years, or maybe the rest of our lives. At worst, we'll be put down. We're going after the man or men who are arguably the wealthiest and most powerful criminals in the world right now, one of whom is widely known to be a dead man. *Please*, baby. I'm begging you. If you're safe, I'll be able to focus only on the job."

She still looked resistant, but he could tell he was wearing her down. She flinched when the distinct clicking noise sounded, signaling that someone was approaching from under the surface. *Thank God Menzies turned the alarms back on*, he thought, not for the first time.

Her eyes widened. "They're here?" she whispered.

He felt the odd calm of the moment when a battle became inevitable come over him. "Not yet, but they're coming. They've crossed the underwater field sensors."

"I don't want to lose you," she said, her eyes shiny. "If I go, can you promise you'll come back?"

His gut was tearing itself in half, one part urging him to lie to get her in the room, the other hating the idea of one more lie between them. "I want to lie, but I think there's been enough of that between us already. I can't promise that, Clo...but I can promise I'll have a better chance of coming back to you."

She flung her arms around him and rose onto her tiptoes to kiss him. She tasted lush, feminine and slightly salty from the two tears that had rolled down her cheeks. "That's enough, then. I love you, Marc."

"Love you, too, Duchess...always," he whispered as she went into the room and locked the reinforced doors from the inside.

Nothing short of a missile blowing up the entire island would be able to hurt her now, and with the amount of reinforcement they'd put into the room, even with a missile, she should probably still be fine, although they'd have to dig it out of the rubble. Marc had every confidence that her brothers would ensure that she was rescued if everything went sideways and he wasn't there to do it—although damn, did he want to be there to do it.

At the sound of the final metallic clink and thud of the locks sliding into place, something in his chest settled. Clothilde was safe. Now he could take care of those who threatened her.

He walked into the darkened kitchen, where he could make out the forms of his teammates. Respect and admiration for the brave men, willing to risk their honor and futures as well as their lives, rose inside of him.

"Barnes, you owe me fifty bucks," Clark said in a low voice.

"I'm good for it," Barnes shot back.

"To be fair, she almost didn't go. Don't know what Casanova here said as his Hail Mary, but I'd like two bottles of it, please," Castellano added, and the men chuckled quietly.

"Can we tell how many tangos we're expecting? ETA?" Marc asked, looking toward Menzies.

"I wouldn't have expected any less from the Gaspards, but damn, you have some fine equipment here. Based on heat signatures on the trackers, looks like fourteen in a submarine, and they know where they're going since they're headed straight for the best place to dock. ETA in about five minutes, so let's do a double-check that we're all locked and loaded, gentlemen."

Marc heard Menzies checking over his equipment, turning off the safety mechanisms, and they did the same thing.

"We still agreed we want these fish alive and wriggling?" Menzies asked.

"Affirmative," Marc answered. "Only exceptions are Carillon and Montfort, and maybe de Sancy if he shows up and resists. Everyone else still on board?"

The chorus of "Yes, sirs" were quiet but firm.

"I'm not gonna get mushy and say that it has been an honor because, shit, I've only got about ten nice speeches in me, so I figure I better save them all for my woman," Marc quipped and heard soft snorts of laughter.

"I'm not buying a bottle of anything from you, man," Clark deadpanned.

There was a long, fraught moment, then Menzies' quiet voice echoed loud in the rock-walled room. "It's go time."

They spread out, into the other rooms of the house, letting the first few intruders make their moves, then neutralizing them with hand- and ankle-cuffs and sound-proof masks. By the relatively bright moonlight, Marc read first confusion on his opponent's face—a military type who looked to be in his early thirties—then recognition. Marc was sometimes recognized by the general public from all of the press after the op during which Cob had been killed, but other service members generally always knew him by reputation. He used the surprise to his advantage, but he wondered if the other man's heart wasn't really in the mission.

Around him, he heard muffled grunts of his teammates taking the others down and dragging them out of the way for questioning later. *Maybe this is going to be easier than we thought*, he said to himself, but regretted it almost instantly when the hostile that Barnes fought with managed to get out a hoarse yell of warning before Barnes subdued him.

"Well, shit on a shingle," Menzies muttered under his breath. They heard the unmistakable sound of a rocket launcher being cocked.

"They wouldn't fire on their own men...would they?" Clark's question answered itself as the projectile connected with the lighthouse wall with a loud thud. If they hadn't been thick stone, reinforced by all the recent work, the wall would have exploded.

"Guess we're gonna have to take this party outside," Marc said with dark humor.

"After you, Prom King," Menzies answered, his smile a white slash in the darkened room.

They had less cover outdoors, but with their knowledge of the terrain, along with some hidden cover zones they'd made sure to add, they took down another group of the intruders.

Crouching, doing a modified crab walk along the rocks, Marc saw Menzies just up ahead, chasing an older man who was fleeing, shooting without accuracy but still dangerously over his shoulder. He winced in sympathy as it looked like a shot winged his CO, but Menzies still took a running leap, catching the man around his knees and taking him down with a loud grunt and thud. Marc remained silent, but inside he cheered when, as soon as Menzies got him into a sitting position to put on the handcuffs, he recognized the prominent nose of Michel Montfort.

"How many are we missing?" he whispered into his earpiece. They all wore them but had been using them very sparingly.

"With the big guy Menzies just took down, I think we're only missing two now." Barnes's voice was steady.

"Anyone have eyes on either of the missing tangos?" Marc whispered, sliding himself over to one of the cover spots. This one had been a naturally occurring overhang, original to the island. In fact, he'd found it so pretty when he'd first scouted the place that he'd imagined taking Clothilde here someday to look at the view. With only two tangos to go, he dared to hope it might be a real possibility now.

As soon as he backed into the alcove, though, he knew he'd made a mistake as a knife slid into his side. He managed to twist at the last second, avoiding the much more damaging blow that it would have been, but the blade still hurt like a son of a bitch.

"Shit…shit. South side of the island. I've got a tango in Blind C," he gasped, feeling wet blood drip down to his waist and along his leg.

He twisted again to defend against the attacker who'd obviously been hiding in wait, and felt a savage satisfaction when his leg connected with something solid, making the other man grunt. The knife fell to the ground with a thud.

"You'll pay for that, *conard*," the man growled, and his voice was barely recognizable as the same as the suave, genteel Armand Carillon he'd met at the gala only a few nights earlier. This man sounded wild, unhinged and absolutely livid.

The swish of fabric gave him away a second before he swiped out again, this time with a smaller knife, but Marc anticipated the blow and blocked it, using his greater brute strength to take it from the older man.

Armand wasn't finished, though, and pulled out a garotte, taking advantage of the small space to lunge onto Marc's back and nearly getting it around his neck by kicking out at Marc's injured side. Again, Marc was able to block the thin wire that could have taken his head off if Armand had had a better grip, although the blows to his knife-wound blazed like they were on fire.

Marc rounded on the older man, his broad shoulders, arms and hands scraping the sides so that he knew he'd have cuts on his knuckles, but he was determined. He leaped forward, bringing the full force of his weight down onto Armand and making him buckle beneath him. It was by no means textbook, or pretty, but he held him there until he heard two sets of footsteps running toward him, and someone thrust a set of handcuffs into his hand so he could clip them onto Armand Carillon.

Breathing heavily — *in fact, shit, why does it feel like my breath is sawing in and out of my lungs?* — Marc extricated himself from the blasted mini-cave to find Clark and Castellano staring at him worriedly.

"Can you pull him out? He tagged my side and it's giving me some trouble," he admitted.

The two younger men had Armand out in next to no time — *damned kids, making it look easy* — and Clark took the older man while Castellano hovered next to Marc as they carefully made their way down the hill.

"How the hell did he surprise you?" Castellano asked.

"He was waiting in the alcove," Marc answered. "It's so hidden, I didn't think anyone would find it easily...rookie move on my part."

"I didn't find it easily, or tonight." Armand practically spat the words at him. "I knew it was there long before you were born, you *fils de putain*. I came here for visits with my lovely Eveline, before my fucking life was stolen from me by Guillaume Gaspard." His eyes blazed with unholy hatred.

"So, in revenge, you became a weapons dealer and a traitor? Sex and drug trafficker?" Marc asked incredulously.

"Ah, *non*...that's just diversification. Well, and for fun, of course." The older man's sudden smile was so genuine that Marc was taken aback by how twisted he seemed.

A sick feeling that he was missing something hit him. He turned to Clark and Castellano as he spoke into his transmitter. "Barnes and Menzies? Did you get the fourteenth man...or do you have eyes on him?"

As he finished, they crested the last outcropping to the flatter surface near the dock. The area was empty, and their comms remained silent. Dread bloomed like a living cloud inside of his chest.

He turned a questioning look at his men. The movement made his cut sting like a bitch, and he knew his grimace didn't entirely hide his wince.

"We left them here with Montfort. I can't imagine both of them leaving without a damn compelling reason." Clark answered his unspoken question.

A slight movement to his side, from the direction of the kitchen door to house, had him spinning so fast pain burned through him, and he had to lean on Castellano.

"I'm afraid there is no fourteenth man," a distinctly feminine voice said, followed by a woman's groan of pain.

# Chapter Sixteen

On her list of least favorite ways to pass the time, Clothilde thought that waiting in a safe room had just moved up to tie with lying in a hospital bed. *Non, in fact, I prefer the hospital bed, because at least then I knew I was doing* something *to recover*, she thought. "Now I'm just sitting here, cut off from everyone else, worried out of my mind that the man I love, who I think may have just told me he loves me, too, is getting killed for me at this very moment." Her words just sort of dropped into the small room, muffled as it was by the walls of reinforced steel.

She *had* promised, though…and she would never want to be the cause of a distraction for Marc. She sat down heavily, trying and failing to gauge how much time had passed. Five minutes? An hour? She would have believed either answer, although she thought it was somewhere in between. *Merde.*

When she heard the faint tapping, at first she thought she'd imagined it. When it came again, louder, but still like a really faint set of three thuds. She excitedly pressed the intercom button.

"Marc? Oh, *mon amour*, I've been so worried!" She wished they'd installed a video camera, too, but Marc had warned her that there had been some issue with it, so the intercom was all she had. In all his urging her to go into the safe room, he'd been very clear that anyone he trusted who came to open the door would know the code word, 'watermelon'.

"It's not Marc...it's me, Élodie. He sent me here to stay with you. Oh, Clo, *mon Dieu*, *Papa*...the things he's been doing! He locked me up, but I got free, and now I'm so afraid of him...afraid of my own father!"

Clothilde recognized her friend's voice instantly, and she could hear the fear in it. She nearly pressed the release button and turned the lever right away, but a sliver of caution made her ask, "Did Marc give you the code word?"

Clothilde heard a faint sniffling, and she could picture her long-time friend, always so delicate and flighty.

"He — he did...but I forgot! It was something silly... oh, Clo, I think I hear them! What if it's one of the men with *Papa*?" Élodie sounded genuinely distressed now, practically wailing, and Clothilde wavered.

She couldn't believe that Élodie could have been lying to her for all the years that she'd known her. Her friend would have had to be an award-winning actress, and frankly, she just didn't think Élodie was capable of it. She was shallow, sure, but charmingly so. And if Élodie had wanted to hurt Clothilde, she'd had countless opportunities to do so. If her father or his men had somehow turned on her — and it sounded like they might have — then Élodie could be in great danger.

With that thought, Clothilde decided she could open the door, but she picked up a heavy paperweight, just in case she was wrong. As Élodie tumbled into the room, bringing the familiar scent of her favorite perfume and lotion and throwing herself against Clothilde in a tearful embrace, Clothilde felt silly for ever having suspected Élodie. She patted her awkwardly with her one free hand.

"It's okay, El. You're safe now. Let's close the door again, then nobody can come in unless we let them," she murmured, turning away from her friend to bend to the lever that would close the door. She was stunned to feel the hard blow to the back of her head, followed by a flash of pain.

As if through a fog, as the world grew dimmer around the edges, she heard Élodie's voice. It was different, now — firmer, harder.

"You always were too trusting, Clo. *Quelle conne*," Élodie said, insulting her intelligence.

Clothilde's last thought before the darkness of unconsciousness claimed her was of Marc. She wished they'd had more time, and she was so sorry she'd let him down — let down the whole team.

\* \* \* \*

"*Clothilde!*" Marc roared, unable to stop the sound when he saw her unmistakable, lithe form on the ground next to Élodie Carillon. Every muscle in his body tensed, ready to do battle.

"If she's groaning, she's alive," Clark whispered into the communicator, and it was just what Marc needed to pull himself back from the red mist of rage that had threatened to consume him.

He took a deep breath. "Where are Menzies and Barnes?" he asked, his tone terse.

Élodie shrugged, picking a piece of lint off her black knit top, even as she held a pistol steady in her other hand, pointed directly at Clothilde. The Carillon daughter's transformation from the flighty, flirtatious society princess at the gala into *this* — a cold, dangerous criminal — was nothing short of astonishing. He could forgive Clothilde for being deceived. He wouldn't have believed it if he weren't seeing it himself. Plus, he had years of painful past experience.

"They're alive...or they were when I tied them up inside with the other useless soldiers. Although, come to think of it, the big guy didn't look so hot. Gunshot wounds, even minor ones, can be a real bitch, don't you think? If I were you, I'd get him some medical attention fast." Her eyes looked like a snake's eyes, glittering and beautiful, but totally devoid of emotion. "Actually, you don't look too great yourself, Constantin." She shot a bright smile in her father's direction. "Well done, *Papa!*"

Armand puffed his chest up. "*Merci, petite.* I've still got some of the vigor I had as a young man left in me, but alas, I find myself in a bit of a bind."

Élodie's tone when she replied was lightly scolding. "I told you we shouldn't have trusted Montfort's men. Hired mercenaries are always *so* much better — the kind of men who will happily murder entire families for the right price, to make a point." She pouted. "You should have let me call Jérôme like I wanted to."

Armand chuckled indulgently, and Marc had the distinct impression that both father and daughter were completely insane. "Such a bloodthirsty little thing, but I'll admit, you may have been right."

Castellano made a slight, stealthy movement and all traces of amusement faded from Élodie's posture.

"Freeze," she ordered, her voice icy and angry. "Unless you want me to shoot Clothilde, which I can tell you, I would find the greatest pleasure in doing. I've been sick of putting up with her for over a decade."

Marc's heart thumped in his chest, in spite of all his outward appearance of calm. "She was your friend," he said, uncomprehending.

Élodie gave him a withering look. "She may have been my friend, but I was never hers. Poor little rich girl... She was lonely and desperate for school companions. Even then, she was nauseatingly sweet, kind to animals and elderly people. If my father hadn't asked me to get close to her, I would have poisoned her food at school and just gotten rid of her then."

"Now, now, *chou-chou*. You've been so good at restraining yourself," Armand said calmingly, and Marc felt a dawning horror. Armand and Michel Montfort were accomplices, but he wondered if he was looking at the true mastermind of the Chimère, a petite blonde capable of deceiving nearly everyone for the majority of her life. Élodie Carillon was obviously a sociopath — and more likely a psychopath.

Élodie blew out a frustrated breath upward, making strands of her golden hair sparkle in the moonlight. "She's just so annoyingly perfect. It was fun...*so much fun*...when Claude made her think he would actually want her. I loved hearing about how much he hurt her and everything he made her do. As if he would choose *her* when he had *me*! She was so fucking provincial about it when she found out he had a lover...stupid cow. He wasn't cheating. He was mine all along."

The pieces clicked into place for Marc. Of course, the attacks on the Gaspard family had started after Clothilde had broken up with Claude. The Carillons and possibly Montfort must have planned on controlling Gaspard Industries somehow through Claude's marriage to Clothilde, but she'd spoiled that.

Clothilde moaned again, and Marc winced at the sly expression that flitted over Élodie's features.

"I could just maim her a little bit…or at least slice her pretty cheeks up so men will stop falling all over themselves for her. She's so helpless." Her laugh was wild. "Do you know, she was *worried* about me? She let me right in when she heard me crying. Stupid fucking bitch."

"*Ma petite belette*," Armand said in a stern but loving tone. "We don't have time for that. We need to get going. The bombs we set are going to go off soon."

Marc, Clark and Castellano exchanged worried looks. Marc knew what they were thinking. They needed to make a move on Élodie, even though they'd be risking Clothilde.

Armand chuckled. "And you're supposed to be the finest? My, my…I can practically hear you thinking. It would be a mistake to harm one hair on my daughter's head, or I can simply press the detonator sewn into my vest and the house will go up like a firecracker, thanks to Élodie's excellent stealth skills. She's always had…unusual passions, including explosives."

"What do you want, then?" Marc growled.

"To get away, of course!" Armand smiled, the expression nearly identical to the social, charming smile he'd worn when Marc had first met him. "You let Élodie and me leave—you can keep Montfort, since he's useless now that you've probably told others about him — and we don't kill all of you right now. Deal?"

"What's to prevent you from setting off the explosives as soon as you're back on your sub?" Marc's jaw was tight, and he knew his words were rough.

"Why, nothing! Only we'd be foolish to set them off when we might still be in range, so you'd better be fast if you want to save anyone...oh, and I do hope you can still swim with that slash I gave you."

They had the fucking Chimère, the triad of people who made up the shadowy entity that Marc had been chasing for years, but he didn't see a way for them to get out of this. It was possible they could get the detonator away from Armand, but there was no guarantee they would find the bombs before any sort of automatic timer ran out, not to mention the risk to Clothilde. At the thought of more harm to his woman, Marc felt a stone in his gut. *Well, shit, we're going to have to trust the insane father-daughter criminal masterminds and let them escape,* he thought.

"*Fuck,*" he breathed, and he saw matching agonized expressions in Clark and Castellano's eyes.

"I see you understand," Armand said with satisfaction, and stepped away from Clark, who begrudgingly loosened his grip.

Carillon-the-elder crooked his arm. "Come along, darling," he said to Élodie.

She looked for all the world like a toddler, reluctant to leave a favorite toy at the playground. "Oh, all right," she agreed, with poor grace.

Although it took everything in him not to lunge at her, Marc held himself back, thinking of all the men in the house. Not only Menzies and Barnes, but the other soldiers, who were likely guilty of nothing more than following orders from a corrupt official.

Just before they reached the door of their submarine, Élodie spoke.

"Just one more thing, though," she said quietly, and spun on her heel with lightning speed to aim her gun back toward them...no, toward *Clothilde*.

Marc leaped to throw his body over Clo's, and at the same time, Clark, who was closer, stepped right into the path of the bullet. It hit him square in the chest and he fell backward, landing hard on the ground. As Marc watched from his position over Clothilde, still protecting her, Castellano ran to Clark. The loud clang of the door to the submarine closing rang out over the sound of the waves.

"How bad is it?" Marc called urgently to Castellano, over the unmistakable sound of the small submarine going under.

"Thank fuck...it hit his vest. He'll have some massive bruising, and breathing is probably gonna hurt for a month, but he's fine." Castellano's relief was obvious, and Clark made a pained sound, as if to punctuate his words.

"Shit...that hurt way worse than I expected," Clark panted. "Bumped my head and knocked the wind right outta me," he finished. "Help me up so we can start to get everyone to the boat."

Castellano held out a hand to him, but Marc only had eyes for Clothilde, injured but thankfully alive underneath him.

"Baby?" he asked, gently touching her cheek. Her eyelashes fluttered but she didn't open her eyes, so he wasn't sure how awake she was. "We gotta go. Gonna lift you because I don't have time to check you out until we're safe." When he touched the back of her head, his hand came away wet with blood, but there didn't seem to be much on the ground so he hoped it wasn't actively bleeding. *Damn Élodie for hitting my Clothilde from behind*, he thought ferociously.

He gathered her into his arms and stood, his side screaming in protest at the pressure. He didn't care. As long as he still had breath in his body, he would take care of his duchess. Still, he nearly toppled when he turned quickly at a splashing sound from the rocks, and he heard Clark and Castellano shift with their weapons as well. The stranger hurriedly tore off his mask.

"Don't shoot!" he said. "I'm friendly...well, sort of, although I'm pissed that my sister looks so injured." He glowered at Marc with the portion of his face that was exposed, which wasn't much in the full coverage wetsuit. Still, Marc recognized him.

"It's Luc Gaspard," he confirmed to his men.

"I'm actually not alone," Luc continued. "I met up with a group, led by Raoul de Sancy, who apparently works for Interpol. Some of them are going to disarm the bombs that Élodie Carillon set in the house, and some of them are going to intercept the sub. We were close enough to hear, but not quite fast enough to get here before Armand and Élodie took off. *Merde, alors*...I never would have guessed that Élodie was involved. *Merde, merde, merde...*"

Marc felt practically limp with relief at Luc's words. "Hold on. They're really going to disarm the bombs and capture the Carillons? How the hell did you '*meet up with*' them?"

Luc's smile was enigmatic. "Haven't you heard? I'm the new head of Gaspard Industries, and one of the wealthiest, most powerful men in the world. I have *friends*, Constantin. And now I think you should set my sister down before you fall over and hurt both of you, er, *more*." Clothilde's youngest brother spoke into some sort of communication device on his wrist. "I need the medic out here, *now*. He sees my sister first, and we have two other wounded, too. Top priority."

Marc allowed himself to sit down into a graceless pile, with Clothilde still cradled in his lap. Her long, dark eyelashes fluttered again as her eyes slitted open.

"Marc?" she whispered.

"I'm here, sweetheart," he answered in a voice gruff with emotion.

"I'm so…sorry." Her voice was a mere thread, and thick with tears.

"God, Clo…don't you *ever* be sorry for being the kind, trusting woman that you are. You amaze me with how open you can still be, even after everything." He held her close until the medic gently forced him to relinquish his grip so they could both be checked out.

# Chapter Seventeen

"Is he going to be okay?" Clothilde asked the doctor who had come in to talk to her and Luc, who sat at her bedside.

The young woman had a reassuring manner. "We ran a few tests because he did some external damage by lifting, uh—"

"By lifting me, I remember," Clothilde prompted when the doctor trailed off uncomfortably.

"Yes, but there was no internal damage, so we just had to do some multi-layered stitching. He's still sedated—mostly because he became rather, er, agitated when he couldn't see you—and he'll be in pain when he comes out of it, but he should be just fine."

"Oh, *Dieu merci*...that's wonderful. I've been so worried," Clothilde breathed, squeezing her brother's fingers so hard that she heard a crack, but Luc didn't complain.

"Do you—?" Luc disentangled his hand from hers with a wince, rising to stand closer to the doctor. "Do you think it would be possible for them to share a room? I know my sister, and she won't take very good care of herself, monitoring for signs of a concussion, staying in bed, unless she can see him for herself."

The doctor gave a surprisingly flirtatious smile, looking suddenly much prettier. "For what you're paying this hospital, you can have a whole wing to yourselves if you want." She looked around the spacious private room. "I'll have a nurse bring Mr. Constantin in here, with a full mobile unit."

After she left, Clothilde flashed Luc a grateful smile. "*Merci, Lu-louche.*"

He smiled, but she thought the crinkles at the corners of his eyes appeared deeper. He looked somehow more careworn, all around, and she wondered if the additional responsibilities he'd taken on lately had been too much.

"It was nothing, Clochette, just making sure my *petite soeur* gets well."

She made a face at him calling her his 'little sister'. "Did you hear an update on Menzies?"

"He's stable. It was minor, as far as gunshot wounds go, and he'll make a full recovery. I also learned through my contacts — well, really just from Raoul de Sancy — that none of the men, including Marc, are going to be charged with insubordination, given the circumstances. It helps that Montfort, along with Armand and Élodie Carillon, are all in secure custody."

Clothilde felt the cold knot of tension inside of her begin to loosen.

"And did you see Brian Clark? How is he?" She shot the rapid-fire questions at her brother, who was unfazed.

Luc nodded. "Naturally...as requested by *mademoiselle*." He gave a fake bow. "They're keeping him for observation overnight in case they missed some internal bleeding, but it looks like he should be just fine. That was incredibly brave of him, stepping in front of a bullet meant for you. I'm thinking of giving him a house, and maybe one for his mom and each of his sisters, too. What do you think?"

Clothilde giggled. "You don't do anything half-assed, do you? I mean, I would mention it to Pierre, but I love the idea!"

"*Ah, non*...you can mention it yourself since he and Marina will be here within the hour."

Clothilde groaned. "Ugh...he's going to hover like a mama bear—and please, *never* tell him I said that. The only one worse is Rémy."

"Did I hear my name?" her second brother said, poking his head into the doorway.

She and Luc exchanged a silent look, then burst out laughing. The movement made her headache worse, and she grimaced.

"Oh *merde*...are you all right? Should I call the nurse? I'm going to find the call button." Rémy said, pushing into the room worriedly with a sheepish-looking Annelise in his wake.

His comment only made Clothilde and Luc laugh harder.

\* \* \* \*

"Are they finally gone?" Marc whispered from the next bed. The fainter light of dawn had just given way to early-morning sunshine, and Annelise and Marina had convinced Rémy and Pierre to go get some rest at a hotel nearby now that they were reassured that their baby sister wasn't dying. Luc had agreed to go as well, somewhat reluctantly, only acquiescing when Barnes and Castellano assured him that they were staying.

Clothilde laughed. "They're gone, although it's likely just a temporary reprieve. How are you feeling?" She looked him worriedly. He'd been more out of it overnight than she'd expected, then he'd had to leave a couple of times to see the doctor and to speak to the other men from his team.

"Much better," he answered reassuringly. "That doc I saw a little while ago confirmed that it was just residual, from the extra sedation. Apparently I was...extremely upset. But now she said I'm pretty much free to go, although no lifting, and I have instructions on the dressing."

A spark of excitement flared in Clothilde's chest. "That's wonderful! And the doctor confirmed earlier that I can leave any time as well, since I didn't have any danger signs."

Marc caught and held her gaze. "Do you want to get out of here, baby?" he asked, and the little flare of hope became bigger, warmer. He was still calling her sweet names, and the things they'd both been so worried about had taken care of themselves.

"So badly," she confirmed, and she pressed the call button for the private nurse her brothers had insisted on. With help from that kind young lady, she and Marc were both ready in record time with discharge papers signed.

Serge, her personal driver, had magically just returned from his long leave—which she now suspected had been Marc's doing—and was going to drive them anywhere they wanted. Feeling like they were escaping from prison, a curious lightness buoyed her as she climbed into the backseat. Marc looked a bit awkward, standing next to the car, as if torn between sitting in the front versus the back seat. She reached out and tugged on his hand.

"Come on," she urged. "Or they'll be back before we can get away!"

His smile was small, but he slid in next to her.

"Where to, Mademoiselle Clothilde?" Serge asked, as he had so many times before, but this time it felt different. *Everything* felt different. She looked over at Marc to see if he was feeling the same thing, but his face wasn't giving much away.

"I thought... There's this seaside resort nearby where I once attended an event, and I just called to reserve us their Presidential Suite, if that's okay?" she finished shyly.

Marc put his hand over hers. "Wherever you want to go, sweetheart," he said, and she thought — *hoped* — it might be a declaration. Something in his expression looked almost nervous, just for a second, but then it was as if she'd imagined it. And why would he be nervous?

"How's your Marie? Patrick and Christiane?" Clothilde asked politely. She did want to know how Serge's family had been — although she also ached to be alone with Marc.

Serge looked her in the rearview mirror as he pulled away from the curb. "They're all well," he said, and his eyes twinkled. "And I won't be offended in the slightest if you want to raise the privacy barrier," he continued with a wink.

She blushed but pushed the button to raise the partition all the same.

"Serge is...almost like an uncle," she explained to Marc. "He went with me to school, although he was quite young then, and he's been with me ever since."

"I can see that he's like family," Marc answered.

There was a long silence, then they both started speaking at once. They stopped, laughing.

"Okay, you first," she said.

He blew out a breath and she realized that her first impression had been correct. He was really nervous about something. Her heart sank. Oh *bon Dieu*, he'd changed his mind. Maybe because she couldn't really make love to him.

"Wait!" she said, holding up her hand. "I, uh, just wanted to say that I would never want to force you to do anything you didn't want to, but I loved every minute we spent together at the lighthouse...well, um, before we were, you know, attacked." She felt horribly awkward, and she knew she was gesturing too much with her hands—she'd practically whapped Marc in the face—but she couldn't seem to stop. "Anyway, I... You bring out emotions, sensations, lots of things I've never felt before, and I want more of that, but I care enough about you to never want you to feel obligated to be with someone who can't, well, perform..."

Marc took her hands gently into his, and his eyes were loving. *Or is he just being kind?* Now she was second-guessing everything.

"Baby...*baby*. I'm not leaving you, especially not because of anything physical that we did, or that we may or may not do in the future. You're gettin' all worked up. I was just feeling nervous because I talked to your brother, asked him for that favor he said he owed me for my pilot friend saving Marina. The favor I requested was his blessing on our relationship."

Clothilde's heart swelled in her chest, warming her to the tips of her fingers and toes.

Marc continued, "Even with Pierre's approval, I know I'll never be good enough for you, but the thing is, I don't think I can live without you, so unfortunately, I think that means you're gonna be stuck with me."

"Oh, Marc...oh, thank goodness. I *want* to be stuck with you. *You're* totally stuck with *me*. I just... What if I can't give you what you need?" She leaned closer. "In *bed*?" she clarified, unsure of why talking about it out loud made her feel so damn uncomfortable.

Marc quirked one side of his mouth up in a half-smile. "Oh, Clo, you have already. You give me everything. But if you want to practice some more with my fingers or something bigger, I'm game right now." His voice went low and sexy on the last word, and just like that, her skin felt sensitive all over.

Her eyes widened. "In a car, not long after dawn, leaving the hospital?"

"Anywhere," he growled, moving closer so he could whisper in her ear. "Always." He was so close, his breath fanned her hair as he spoke, and she gave a delicate shiver. "How far away is this place?" he asked, putting his hand on her thigh. It was warm, even through the fabric of her jeans. She sent a mental thank-you to both Marina and Annelise, who'd both thoughtfully brought her a couple of outfits from home or she would have had to check out in a hospital gown or dirty clothes.

"Close," she whispered.

"Not close enough," he rumbled, covering her mouth with his. He tasted like mint toothpaste with a hint of his own spice, and she'd never tasted anything better. His outdoor-fresh scent surrounded her, although it was tempered by a slight antiseptic note, and she put her arms around his neck to draw him closer. When he moved to lift her onto his lap, she batted his hand away.

"Oh, no! The doctor said no lifting," she scolded, then blushed. "I'll climb up myself...very gently."

Before she could suit words to actions, the car slowed to a stop.

"Thank God," Marc said. "Longest car ride *ever*."

She let out a burst of laughter at his exaggeration. "It was only ten minutes!"

"Ten minutes too long," he returned, stealing another kiss. "Ten minutes I could have been nibbling on your lips." He nipped her bottom lip. "Or your beautiful nipples," he continued, tweaking one and making her gasp. "Or your hot little pussy," he finished, reaching out his hand but she was ready this time and blocked him.

"*Ah, ben, non, monsieur!*" she admonished, pursing her lips and making the clicking noise that all French-speaking parents made when their children were naughty...or their overeager hunk boyfriends. "Serge will see!"

"All right, all right...I'll wait five more minutes, but not one more second, so you'd better pray check-in doesn't take long. In five minutes, this hand –" He gestured with his right hand, with its long, strong fingers, capable of giving so much pleasure. "This hand will be inside your panties, no matter where we are, so I suggest you hurry."

Laughing, she practically tumbled out of the door as Serge opened it and took off for the check-in desk at a fast clip, almost a run but not quite. She heard Marc's steps behind her, then Serge's snort of amusement.

# Chapter Eighteen

They'd just closed and locked the door to their room when the five minutes were up. Marc had to admit he was almost disappointed, since he'd been envisioning feeling Clothilde up in the elevator or even in the corner of the hotel lobby, but he hadn't reckoned with the alacrity with which people moved when VIPs like Clothilde — or any of the Gaspards — arrived. The woman at the check-in desk had practically bounced on her heels, she'd been so eager to assist them.

Still, it had been fun to watch his woman squirm, hurrying so that pink flags of color bloomed on her cheeks. Even now, she was breathing rapidly, standing in the center of their room. 'Room' was too modest a word for the palatial suite. It was the entire top floor of the resort, set right on a pristine North Atlantic beach, and behind Clothilde he could see that there was an enormous private balcony with a full dining table and what looked to be an enormous hot tub or small pool. What he liked the look of most, though, was the oversized California king bed he spied through an open door in the corner.

"Your five minutes are up, sweetheart. I need to feel you *now*." He'd meant to tease her, but he realized it was true. They'd nearly died. It had been so close. Now that he had her alone, at last, he wanted to celebrate.

He went to her and hugged her, hard, pressing against her softness but also reassuring himself that she was okay...solid.

She seemed to sense the change in his mood. "Are you all right?"

"I almost lost you yesterday," he said, his voice going hoarse. "Never again, baby. God, I love you...so much."

Her eyes snapped up to his in surprise, and he cursed himself. It was the first time he'd said the words in a way that she was sure to hear them. Her dark eyes looked shiny, filled with tenderness...and something deeper.

"Oh, Marc," she breathed, lifting to her tiptoes to kiss him. What started as a sweet gesture quickly morphed into something darker, more primal. He devoured her with his mouth, and ran his hands up and down her back, squeezing her lush ass, stroking her silky hair. She didn't smell like her usual shampoo, but her warm, womanly scent was still amazing. He trailed kisses down her cheek over to nip her earlobe, then down her elegant neck to lick along her collarbone. She let her head fall back and her posture of trust, of surrender, not only to him but to pleasure, made his cock swell and strain against the zipper of his pants.

He ground his hips against her to relieve the pressure, but instead, the feel of her soft curves, along with her sexy little sounds of appreciation, only served to further inflame his desire. He growled with frustration when he remembered that he wasn't supposed to pick her up and carry her to the bedroom, but he contented himself with slowly walking her backward, punctuating each step with a kiss. After five steps, he pulled off her thin, flowy blouse-thing, exposing her white lace bra, which was like a gorgeous frame for the creamy swells of her breasts. After five more steps, he paused to undo her jeans and pull them down and off her legs, kissing bare skin on his way to stand back up.

Her panties were white lace, too, and he could see her dark thatch of curls through the fabric.

"So fucking beautiful, Duchess...you're like a goddamn angel, and I'm sure I shouldn't be the one who gets to touch you, but I swear I'm gonna make you feel so good, like my queen," he breathed.

She shook her head emphatically, making her long, dark hair move like a shining waterfall around her bare shoulders. "No...not a queen. When I'm in public, I'm playing a role, serving my family and our business. You make me feel like a woman, and a lady—and *loved*."

"You are that," he agreed. "Now go lie down on that giant bed so your man—and you can feel free to treat me like a king—can taste you," he ordered, and he marveled again at the clear gleam of interest that lit her eyes when he got bossy with her.

With a saucy toss of her hair, she went to the expansive bed and stretched out. He stalked slowly over to her, taking his own clothing off as he went. She watched him avidly, and her attention made him move more sinuously, putting on a show if his duchess liked it that much. When he pulled off his pants and underwear together, leaving himself naked and his cock huge and throbbing, pointing toward her, she gave a little '*ooh*' of excitement and bit her lower lip in a sexy gesture that he knew had to be unconscious.

"Take off your bra and panties, baby," he commanded, partly because he wanted to see her do it, and partly because he wasn't sure his hands wouldn't betray him by trembling if he did it himself.

She unclipped her bra first, freeing her generous breasts and making her nipples pebble in the cool morning air. His throat went dry. Next, she shimmied out of her panties, and he didn't think that anything had ever been sexier than her shy smile as she lay there, utterly nude, with the light just barely glinting at the moisture on her dark curls at the juncture of her thighs.

"Glorious...fucking stunning, Clo," he said reverently. "You ready for me to lap up all that honey from your sweet pussy?"

Clothilde nodded. "Oh, yes," she said, with endearing eagerness so that he practically leaped onto her.

Her taste was just as addictive as he remembered, like fucking ambrosia, and he reached his hands up to stroke her sensitive breasts at the same time. At the dual sensations, she tightened her thighs around his ears, muffling the sounds until all he could hear were her squeaks and moans, along with the wet sounds of him loving her with his mouth.

"Are you ready for me to put my fingers inside you again?" he asked, the question vibrating right against her slit because he couldn't move too much. She shivered and gasped.

"Yes, *oui*, please...put them inside me. Feels so good, Marc," she panted.

His first finger slid in much easier than the first time, and his second finger went in, too, its passage eased by her wet arousal.

"Here comes the third, Clo... Get ready," he warned, and his dick nearly exploded when she let her legs fall open.

"Please," she moaned. "I want to be ready for you, *j'ai si besoin de toi*, need you inside me so badly. I trust you," she said.

Her confidence humbled him, and he vowed silently never to betray such a precious gift. He put his third finger inside her and bent to lick her again, swirling his tongue around her sensitive bundle of nerves and humming, just a little, so that she came so hard that she squeezed around him and arched her back, nearly bowing right off the bed. He drew out her pleasure for as long as possible until her breathing began to slow again.

"I think you liked that," Marc teased in a gravelly voice, and Clothilde realized that she still squeezed his fingers in her channel.

"So amazing, the way you kissed me, and inside me...it's like nothing else," she admitted. "I want to make you feel the same way," she continued. "Tell me what you like best?"

Marc levered his arm so he could stretch out next to her, pulling his fingers from her, making her suck in a sharp breath and feel curiously lonely.

"That's a beautiful offer, baby...and I love it, but the answer is easy. I like everything you do. Just like last time, my body is yours to explore, and nothing you want to try is ever gonna be wrong." He leaned back and grinned, putting his arms behind his head and making his biceps bulge. "You can climb up here and ride my face if you want to, or bite my chest, or just look at my balls. It's all good because *you'll* be doing it."

His words made her laugh, and her tension dissipated. Actually, she loved the idea of riding his face, so she tucked it away for later.

"Look at your balls, huh?" she prompted.

He nodded.

"They are fine-looking, to be sure...but what if I want to touch them?" She took a deep breath, feeling daring. Marc had proven himself to her in the lighthouse, so she hated that she needed reassurance...but she did. If they were going to try to go further, which she wanted, she had to be certain. "You won't force me to do anything?"

"*Never.*" His answer was swift and decisive. "I'll keep my hands behind my head this time, even if it kills me, and I won't so much as thrust my hips."

She felt the same rush of power as she had before, to have such a huge, dominant warrior—a hero, *her* hero—at her mercy. Her core went liquid at the idea of kissing and sucking his cock again, which rose, thick and long, from the light-colored curls at its base.

"I want to stroke and kiss you everywhere this time," she said, leaning down to gently nip one of his nipples.

He gasped, but he didn't move his hands. "Absolutely," he answered in a strangled voice.

"But most of all, I want to climb on top and ride you...to see how you feel inside me." She punctuated her statement with a long caress along the length of his dick, rubbing her finger into the drop of silky pre-cum that beaded on the tip, then bringing it to her mouth.

Marc made an inarticulate grunting sound that was somewhere between a wheeze and gurgle, but still sexy. Better yet, he didn't move his hands, although his biceps looked molded in stone.

She'd known it was safe, but he'd just reaffirmed it, so she took her time, stroking his sides although avoiding the small white dressing over his wound. She explored his body like her own personal playground, feeling the soft but springy hairs on his arms and legs, cataloging his many scars. She kissed his neck and hands, tasting her own flavor on his fingers, and looked at and stroked his surprisingly velvety balls.

When she bent her head to take him into her mouth, he sighed and grunted.

"Oh, God, baby, so good," he encouraged.

She circled his thickness with her hands and swirled her tongue around the tip until he looked like he might lose his mind. She grew bolder, taking part of his length into her mouth and throat.

"Fuck, oh, that's so fucking good. I won't be able to last if you keep doing that," he warned, his voice hoarse with intensity. "If you wanted to come up and use my mouth to suck on your pert little nipples for a minute, you might like that."

Clothilde felt her channel clench at his suggestion, and she reluctantly released his cock to crawl up the bed, leaning down so Marc could suck one eager little bud into his mouth. He felt hot, and her nipples were still sensitized from his earlier attention, so it didn't take long for her to start squirming against him. When he moved to the other nipple, pulling it into his mouth and circling his tongue around and around the tip, finally nipping it gently, she was undulating her hips against him.

She felt a brief hesitation before moving to straddle his hips, but then she looked down at him. His face was fierce, set in a mask of desire so intense he nearly appeared grim, but there was tenderness in his eyes. He was rigid with need—not just his magnificent cock but his whole posture—but he held himself back, for *her*. This man, her Marc, would *never* hurt her.

"You look so fucking sexy right now, Clo. I can't even tell you how much you're turning me on," he said in a low voice, and his deep tone and the emotion behind it made goosebumps rise all over her skin.

She positioned herself over him and slid onto the first few inches of his length. He was thicker than her ex, so she felt an extra fullness, but not in a scraping or bad way.

"Ooh," she said in appreciation as she lowered the next few inches. Underneath her, Marc held himself completely still, as if ready to pull out and stop at any second, and deep love for him, along with respect for his honor, swelled inside her.

She lowered herself the last few inches, until she felt his hip bones against her inner thighs and he couldn't go any deeper. She felt amazingly full, and closer to Marc than she'd ever been to anyone.

He groaned, a low, sexy sound of pure pleasure.

"You feel like heaven, sweetheart. Like fucking paradise."

She gave an experimental wiggle of her hips, making both of them gasp.

"You're so big, and thick," she admitted. "I like it, though… It feels good everywhere inside."

"Thank God," Marc breathed.

Clothilde began to rotate her hips, finding a rhythm that seemed to drive them both crazy, and Marc reached up to tease her nipples.

"Clo, holy shit, the sight of you riding me is sending me close to the edge." His voice was strained, and indeed, his eyes held something wild.

Clothilde reveled in her power, in her femininity and in the sensations between them. She could feel her own orgasm building again, but she needed something more.

"Thrust up into me. You can move your hips," she said, and as if she'd unleashed a madman, Marc began to push into and out of her with purpose so that she could only hold on to his shoulders for dear life as waves of pleasure radiated from his every motion. As he increased his speed, she tightened around him, and when he bucked up with an exultant cry, releasing jet after jet of hot semen deep inside her, the sensation sent her careening into pure bliss as well. Her channel rippled and tightened around his length, pulling more liquid from him until they were both shuddering and spent, with her collapsed on his sweaty chest.

She felt like one giant puddle of pleasure — or rather, like a combined puddle, because she could no longer tell where she ended and Marc began — and she loved it. She wanted to stroke his chest, but it was almost too much effort to contemplate lifting her hand from where it felt like it might be stuck there. The most she could do was dart out her tongue to lick his skin, which tasted spicy and salty. His chest rose and fell beneath her in a slowing cadence, and the thump-thump of his heartbeat was steady underneath her, blending with the muted sound of the waves outside, gentler than the waves on the cliffs at Wilson's Rock.

When she finally felt recovered enough to speak, she said into his pectoral muscle, "Are you alive? Because I'm not sure I am." She gave just one belly laugh — the extent of her physical power — before continuing. "Is it possible to die from pleasure? Death from dicking?" She giggled. "Croaking by cocking?"

Marc's answering chuckle was deep and rich and rolled through her body as well, given how intimately they were still connected. "I would happily concede that our truly spectacular lovemaking could have killed both us, if it weren't for how cold my toes feel from a draft coming in from the window."

Clothilde peeled her cheek off his skin, and half-raised herself on her arm enough to look at Marc. The tender expression on his face, along with the soft emotion blazing from his eyes, made her heart feel suddenly too large for her chest. She reached out one arm and flipped half of the duvet over them before snuggling back down into Marc's arms.

"Feel like a king yet?" she teased.

Marc answered her seriously. "Every damn day with you, Clo. Every one."

They were silent for a long moment, but it was the comfortable silence of lovers content to just be.

It was Marc who spoke again. "So, I sort of hinted at it in the car, but...how'd you like to wake up like this for the next fifty or sixty years? I've been thinking of taking a step back from the security business, cutting down to just one client. I'm not much of a bargain for someone like you."

He spoke casually, but Clothilde could hear the real emotion behind his question. She sat up, letting the blanket slither down off her shoulder, uncaring of anything but looking at him.

"Are you serious? Are you...? Is this a proposal? Because if not, it's a bit late to try to talk me out of falling for you." She was torn between caution and elation.

"If you have to ask, it's not a very good one, huh?" he quipped. "Yes, my love, my woman, my everything... Will you marry this soon-to-be-retired hero?"

"*Oui*! Yes!" Clothilde cried, leaning down to kiss his mouth. "But, *mon amour*, you'll always be my hero."

"I can live with that," he answered, grinning, and kissed her back.

# Want to see more from this author? Here's a taster for you to enjoy!

## Minne-sorta Falling in Love: Mac of All Trades
### Aurora Russell

### *Excerpt*

"I have to admit that I'm impressed by how well you handled all the questions from the police about Brock Templeton," Lana said grudgingly. Joe 'Mac' MacKenzie was already much too cocky, and his ego hardly needed any stroking. Watching him with the officers, though, had been like watching a master. She could easily see how he'd earned so many promotions and honors as a Navy pilot.

He shrugged, not taking his hands off the wheel, but the small smile he gave—*and why couldn't he be a little less handsome?*—was self-satisfied. "It's the accent," he answered, really laying it on thick. "Like my daddy said, a Southern man tells the best jokes and is always welcome at any dinner table or gatherin'."

She snorted, and not the usual elegant sniff that sometimes escaped but a full-on nasal rattling noise. "You sound like Tom Hanks' cousin from the deeper South—like, the Mariana Trench of Alabama."

"Oh, no, ma'am, not Alabama—perish the thought! My family's pure Georgia. How did you guess I was from Mariana Trench, though?" he teased. "My granddaddy was mayor of Mariana Trench, as a matter of fact."

She raised one skeptical eyebrow. "Matter of fact, *eh*?"

Her heart felt like it beat double-time at Mac's charming grin, flashing like the Cheshire Cat's as it was lit periodically by the streetlights they passed. *Lana Fitzhugh, you of all people know better than to get your head turned by a handsome, charming man*, she scolded herself. He'd shown himself to be overbearing, jealous and possessive when he'd fired one of the caterers on the spot earlier in the evening without even consulting her. *But you didn't disagree with his decision*, the annoyingly honest voice in the back of her head forced her to acknowledge. The caterer had actually been making her uncomfortable, but it had been *her* problem to deal with, not Mac's.

"Would I lie to such a stunning creature? You wound me, ma'am, straight to the core." He pretended to be hit by a bolt to the heart, and she couldn't help the burble of laughter that she tried to stifle. He was just so ridiculous. He was smart, funny and seemed truly dedicated to helping other men and women who'd recently left the service. Several times over the past few weeks as she'd worked closely with him to plan that night's fundraiser, she'd found herself liking him in spite of her better judgment.

The party had been an unqualified success for the worthy veteran's charity that Mac and Fitz, her second-oldest brother, had become very involved with. *Well*, she mentally amended, *it was practically perfect until Brock Templeton, Fitz's fiancée's ex-boyfriend, made a scene, insulted Clara and drunkenly confessed to trying to cause her to 'accidentally' lose their baby*. Brock had clammed up when they'd gotten to the police station, but, thank goodness, Mac had already recorded everything on his phone.

"I know that Fitz and Clara will really appreciate your getting the police to agree to take their statements tomorrow. They don't like to leave baby Hope for too long," she answered, sobered by the recollection of the night's events.

"I'm certain they've checked in on Miss Hope, but I do believe they may be doing some, uh, private celebrating of their engagement, too—or, at least, on behalf of lonely single dudes everywhere, I *hope* they are. It's not every day that a man gets the woman he loves to agree to marry him." Mac's voice was light, but there was something sad behind his tone, just below the surface.

"No…no, it's not," she agreed, snapping her mouth shut when she realized she sounded wistful. She had plenty to be grateful for, especially now that Fitz had returned to their lives, bringing the lovely Clara and Hope, shaking up the household and breaking their oldest brother, Drew, and Lana herself out of the cold, boring routines they'd fallen into. "Clara is just lovely—and Hope, too. I couldn't be happier for them," she enthused, perhaps a bit too heartily.

Mac quirked one side of his mouth up in a wry smile. "You've convinced me…but are you sure you've convinced yourself?"

His insight surprised her.

"I suppose you're right…but please don't think it's about Clara, because she really is wonderful. I truly am happy for them." She paused, forcing herself to be truthful. "Maybe a little envious, too. A long time ago — *God*, when I was so young and arrogant, self-assured to the point of naiveté and convinced of my own completely irresistible self—I made some really awful decisions."

If he'd said anything, she probably wouldn't have continued, but he remained silent, waiting.

"I ended up with a badly trampled heart—let's call it pulverized instead of broken—and it cost me my best friend and years of my relationship with Fitz, too." Suddenly uncomfortable with just how much she'd revealed, she gave a weak laugh. "I'm sorry I said that...*burdened* you with that. You didn't ask for my life story."

Mac touched his hand to her thigh for an instant before returning it to make a hard turn with the steering wheel. "Whatever happened, it sounds like you learned a lot from it, although I'm sorry it sounds like it caused you so much pain," he replied in a low, earnest voice, so different from the light, teasing tones he usually used with her. "And, Lana, nothing you could ever tell me would be a burden," he finished, clearing his throat. She wondered if he was equally uncomfortable with what she'd revealed.

Taking pity on him, she deliberately lightened the tone. "I bet you say that to all the young debutantes," she answered. "Does it ever work?"

Mac's laughter was a surprised bark. "*Touché*, Miss Fitzhugh. It might shock you to learn that I have, indeed, known my fair share of debutantes, including my two sisters."

"Now, that *is* unexpected," she agreed, although now that she pictured it, she could definitely see Mac all dressed up in a gray afternoon suit, flirting shamelessly and fetching lemonade for some pretty young thing. "Does that mean you can dance? You never asked me once tonight."

They stopped at a signal so that his face was half in the light and half out, but the expression on the half she could see was distant. The silence between them became thick and uncomfortable. Lana knew she must have mis-stepped, but she wasn't certain how.

"I don't think I can dance anymore — or at least not like I used to," he answered at last, his voice gruff. "I lost my right leg below the knee about eighteen months ago now."

Lana sucked in a sharp breath. She'd known Mac and Fitz had met in a military hospital, and she'd noticed that Mac walked with a limp, but she'd never wanted to pry, figuring that Mac would tell her about his injury if he wanted her to know. She'd never imagined he'd lost part of his leg entirely.

"Horrified? Tempted to feel sorry for me?" Mac sounded defensive. "I've had to deal with just about every type of reaction."

She touched his shoulder gently. "Nope, just surprised, since I didn't know," she answered quietly. "I can't even begin to understand how difficult recovering from an injury like that would be, and I admire your charity work even more now."

The enclosed space of the small front seat of the car felt suddenly intimate, especially so late at night, as if the two of them might be the only people awake in the city — or maybe in the world.

They pulled onto the long driveway — well, really a small, private lane — that led to the main house of her family's compound — Fitzhugh's Folly, as it was widely known, given how outrageously expensive and ostentatious it had been when her grandfather, Pat, had built it.

Tonight, it looked cavernous and dark...forlorn. *Or maybe that's just me*, Lana thought, but recognizing the source of her melancholy didn't make her feel better. Her oldest brother, Drew, had opted to stay at his high-rise apartment downtown to save time before his morning meeting. Her grandfather and Roger, who was ostensibly their butler but really a member of the family, along with being her grandfather's long-time companion and probably his closest friend, had gone to bed early, so the lights had likely been out in their wing since ten o'clock or so.

Fitz and Clara were staying in the large separate guest house — which was actually the original house on the property — so Lana would be alone in the north wing of the main house. She should have been comfortable with it — in fact, she *was* very used to it, since at least three or four nights a week she had the mansion practically to herself, with its multitude of bedrooms, sitting rooms and other various spaces for practically every conceivable purpose. She often relished the solitude, after needing to be 'on' for so much of her charity work, which was no easy feat for a natural introvert who would have been happy just reading and drinking tea. Tonight, though, she felt a pang of loneliness.

Before she knew it, they'd pulled up to her front doors. They were tall, made from a thick, dark wood, and the whole impressive entryway looked forbidding, shrouded in darkness.

"They don't leave the front lights on for you?" Mac asked, breaking the silence and some of the tension.

Lana wished they did, but they weren't that kind of family. "I often get home late, and my grandfather is surprisingly frugal, so…" She shrugged, looking away. "I'm accustomed to it." She could feel Mac's gaze, but she refused to turn toward him. "I go in the side door, anyway."

Before she could tell him not to, Mac had gotten out of the car and come around to open her door, offering her his arm. He still looked impossibly handsome in the fading moonlight. It was so cold at the tail end of mid-November that his breath puffed out of his mouth in white clouds, but he looked unruffled in his pristine dress uniform.

"Let me walk you there?" he asked. When she hesitated, with one leg on the ground and one still in the car, he spoke again. "So I'm certain you're safe."

With a swift bolt of comprehension, Lana realized he must be doing this — ensuring her safety — for Fitz, as a favor to her brother, which made total sense. They hadn't totally repaired their relationship as brother and sister, since that would take a long time, but they'd made some good headway, and Fitz had always been protective of her when they had been younger. *So why do I feel so disappointed?* she wondered.

"Since you insist," she agreed, unable to keep the snap of annoyance from her voice entirely. Still, holding onto Mac's solid, warm arm, inhaling his distinctive scent, so smooth and comforting, like masculine soap and cinnamon and detergent, she wasn't sorry not to be alone. No…it was more than that. She wasn't sorry that Mac was the specific man she walked with.

Across the lawn, she saw a light come on in the guest house, which she recognized was in baby Hope's room. Silhouetted on the shades, she saw a curvy woman's figure rocking a child, and a larger outline as a man came up behind her, enveloping them in his shadow with a hug and leading them away from the window. The peace and serenity of the domestic scene, along with recollections of the love that she'd seen on their faces every time Fitz and Clara looked at each other and at tiny, perfect Hope, made her heart hurt, because she knew she would never have anything like it—and didn't deserve it, anyway. Tears filled her eyes. As their steps slowed when they neared the side entrance to her area of the house, she kept her face averted from Mac so he wouldn't see.

"I'm here safely, so you can report back to Fitz that you did your duty," she answered, more coldly than she'd intended.

"Hey, now," Mac answered, turning toward her in front of the side steps and urging her chin up with one strong but gentle finger so he could look at her face. "I never do anything I don't want to do—not anymore, in any case—and I wanted to see you to your door safely for myself, so *I* wouldn't worry." He studied her, and she had the uncomfortable sensation that he saw much more than she'd wanted. "Are those tears, sugar?"

"No," she denied in a thick voice, but her body immediately betrayed her as two droplets fell from her lashes and traced icy paths down her cheeks.

"Oh, darlin', I'm sorry. Not quite sure what I did or said, but I never meant to make you cry," he murmured in a deep, sincere voice, and Lana thought that she could have forgiven him just about anything, if there'd been something to forgive.

"It's not you," she answered. "It's just that I feel so...*alone* sometimes, you know?" she admitted.

"God, yes," he replied, with feeling. He wrapped his arms around her and pulled her close into his body, so tightly that something he had pinned to his uniform pressed into her cheek. In spite of the tiny prick of pain, she felt safer and warmer than she had for a long, long while. "You're not alone now, Lana."

She tipped her head back, and she wasn't sure whether she pushed up toward him first or he lowered his head, but somehow he closed his mouth over hers, and it was sublime. At first, his lips were gentle—surprisingly soft for such a brave, tough ex-military pilot—but when she moaned, he deepened the kiss, and she savored his spicy taste, a little like the coffee they'd drunk at the police station, but mostly just his own unique flavor.

She pushed herself against him, feeling his hardness rise, thick and long, against her stomach, and he tangled his hands into her updo, dislodging bobby pins, which made tiny metallic pings as they landed on the steps. He caressed her tongue with his, claiming her mouth in bold strokes until her nipples tightened against his chest as she imagined how he would claim her with other parts of his body.

When he finally raised his mouth from hers, his breathing harsh and uneven, she noticed they must have walked together right up to the wall of the house, and her back was cold against the bricks. The rapid puffs of her breath mingled with the clouds of his, and he leaned his forehead against hers.

"I'm sorry... I got a little carried away," Mac said, and they still stood so close that she could feel the quick rise and fall of his chest against her breasts.

"No, no...I was just as into it, maybe more," she said, then flushed with embarrassment. "I didn't mean...well, you know. I'm sure you could tell that I was enjoying it, but of course we shouldn't have done that."

Mac took a step back. "What do you mean?"

Lana bit her lip, feeling like she wished the ground would swallow her up. Where was some handy quicksand when you needed it?

"Well, like you said, I'm sorry, too."

Mac shook his head. "No, darlin', I'm not sorry it happened...only sorry we went so fast."

When she looked up into his face—so handsome, perfectly formed with strong lines and eyes that she couldn't make out clearly right now in the low light but that she knew were a startling deep green and probably blazing with emotion—she wished she dared to trust herself again with a good man, a kind man, a true friend like Mac. Being with someone like him wasn't in the cards for her, though. That kind of man wanted more than she could give—more than she was capable of giving anymore.

She put her hand on his chest. "Mac, there can't be anything more between us. I can't be with someone like you." She tried to be gentle, but she rushed her words as thick tears rose in her throat.

Mac took another step back, breaking all contact between them. "Someone like me, huh? Why did I think you were different?" His voice was hollow, resigned...but the tone was underlaid with hurt.

"That's not—" she started to explain, but he cut her off.

"You know what, Lana? Don't say anything you might regret. I'll stay away from you, and you can stay away from me from now on, but no matter what, we'll still have to see each other sometimes, and I don't want it to be any worse than it has to be."

Lana felt as if he'd slapped her, but she forgave him for lashing out. He didn't understand, but explaining might make it more painful. As Fitz's closest friend, he *was* bound to cross her path in the future at important events.

"If that's what you want," she agreed, her voice low and sad.

"Does it matter what I want?" Mac's laugh was mirthless, and he started to turn away. "No, hold on. I'm gonna say one more thing first, because I vowed that if I ever started to feel for someone again, I would say the words out loud — not leave confusion or doubt."

Lana braced herself for whatever he was going to say, but his words were more surprising for their tenderness than anything else.

"It sounds like we don't feel the same way and maybe you won't thank me for saying this, but no matter how you feel, I care about you. I was beginnin' to think I might be able to care pretty deeply and that maybe you could, too."

She winced at the raw tone of his voice.

"That doesn't change overnight. Truth is, for a man like me, that doesn't really change, *period*. So if you're ever in trouble or hurting — no matter everything we said tonight — you can call me and I'll be there. That's it."

His offer stunned her, and letting him turn around and walk away, back into the darkness that was beginning to streak gray with the first light of the coming dawn, was one of the worst things she'd ever forced herself to do. He'd be better off without her, though. She knew it, and he'd recognize it, too, in time.

She'd thought her sad, shredded heart was incapable of feeling anything anymore, but now she learned — too late — that she must have been mistaken. If it had truly been destroyed, it couldn't hurt so darn bad now. She hurried inside the massive house, her steps echoing off the walls and floors of the empty rooms, and cried for everything that might have been.

# About the Author

Aurora is originally from the frozen tundra of the upper-Midwest (ok, not frozen all the time!) but now loves living in New England with her real-life hero/husband, two wonderfully silly sons, and one of the most extraordinary cats she has ever had the pleasure to meet. But she still goes back to the Midwest to visit, just never in January.

She doesn't remember a time that she didn't love to read, and has been writing stories since she learned how to hold a pencil. She has always liked the romantic scenes best in every book, story, and movie, so one day she decided to try her hand at writing her own romantic fiction, which changed her life in all the best ways.

Aurora loves to hear from readers. You can find her contact information, website details and author profile page at https://www.totallybound.com

Home of Erotic Romance

Sign up for our newsletter and find out about all our romance book releases, eBook sales and promotions, sneak peeks and FREE romance books!